DEATH TIDE

J.E. TRENT

Edited by
JUDITH SHAW

Edited by
EILA TRENT

BONUS

Get the free prequel and new release notifications.
https://readerlinks.com/l/965413

1

E rica lay in bed on her back, panting for a few minutes before she rolled to her side and reached for her cigarettes on the nightstand. She lit one and took a long drag and savored the satisfaction of hot sex and a smoke.

Charles scooted up on his back against the headboard, his face wrinkled as he said, "That's a disgusting habit. I wish you wouldn't smoke around me," as he waved the smoke away from his face.

"That's rich coming from you. Maybe you should try taking a look in the mirror when it comes to having a disgusting habit, as she looked at the spoon and syringe on the nightstand next to him."

She took a couple deeper drags then crushed the tip of the cigarette in the ashtray.

For the past six weeks, she and Charles had rendezvoused at the Royal Kona resort every Wednesday in the afternoon. She tried to time it when she thought her husband Larry was at the King Kam hotel screwing his mistress on the other side of the village.

"We have to talk," Erica said as she reached for her bra and panties on the floor and started to put them on.

"About what?"

"About us, we can't do this anymore."

"Why?" Charles asked as he rolled out of bed and pulled on his jockey shorts.

"I have a feeling Larry's having me followed. As much as I've enjoyed our playtime together, I can't afford to ignore my gut on this. If he finds out you and I have been screwing, at best he'll divorce me. I'll be out on the street with nothing because I signed a prenup. At worst, he'll kill me."

Charles didn't say anything as he continued to put his clothes on. After combing his hair he looked in the mirror to make sure it was perfect, then sat on the chair in the corner of the room. He stared at the ocean through the sliding glass door before choosing his words.

"It was fun. Now we're over, is that how it's going to be?" he said as he didn't make eye contact and continued looking at the water.

"Pretty much," she fired back as she picked up her purse and headed to the door.

"Stop right there!" Charles ordered. "Sit down, we're not done here," as he pointed at the couch.

Erica stopped and turned, "Ok, make it quick, I have to be someplace in fifteen minutes."

"I'm going to need some incentive to remain discreet," he said as he picked at his fingernails.

Her forehead puckered as she said, "Let me see if I got this straight. You're going to tell my husband you've been screwing me if I don't pay you to keep your mouth shut? You know, he'll kill you, right?"

"I don't think so. I'm going to tell him you were doing somebody else–the other guy you've been screwing. Remember? The young real estate agent with that new firm from Honolulu that recently set up shop out at the Four Seasons Resort. Tanner is what I seem to recall him saying his name was."

Erica's eyes grew wide open as Charles continued,

"He seems like a real nice fellow. I met him once after I spotted him and you together in the parking lot of the Four Seasons. I would have thought nothing of it if he hadn't leaned in the window of your car and slid his tongue down your throat. So, being the inquisitive sort that I am, I followed him back to the bar and struck up a conversation. He's a rather chatty fellow after he's had a couple of drinks. I mentioned I'd seen him earlier kissing a beautiful woman; he looked around the room of the bar and said shhh. It only took a couple of more drinks before he was happy to share some of the fun the two of you had been having."

Her eyes bored into his for a moment before she whipped open her handbag and pulled out her checkbook. "How much asshole," she said, gritting her teeth as she held the pen ready to write the check.

"I don't know yet. I'll give you a number when I have one. I need a couple of days to think about it."

Erica shoved the checkbook back into her purse, and glared at Charles for a moment before she stormed out of the room.

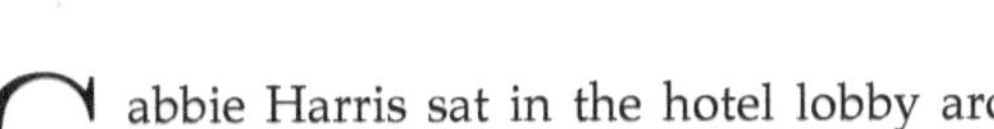

Gabbie Harris sat in the hotel lobby around the corner from the elevator. Erica's intuition was right, Larry Black had hired Gabbie two weeks earlier because he suspected Erica of cheating. Never mind the fact that he had a mistress.

Gabbie heard the loud click clack of stiletto heels coming her way long before she could see Erica round the corner. She turned on the stealth video camera sitting in a briefcase on the floor next to her and picked up a newspaper, focusing her attention on it as Erica quickly walked by. Gabbie clicked off the remote to the camera and sighed. Erica and Charles had been smart enough to never be seen together in public and getting a video or photo of them together had so far proven difficult.

Charles exited the elevator a few minutes later and Gabbie watched him walk toward the parking lot as she shook her head in disgust. "I'll get you my pretties," she murmured to herself.

Jessica's voice crackled through Gabbie's earpiece, "Did you get it?"

Gabbie pushed the mic button on her two-way radio, "No."

"Me either, she's already left the lot and I can see him walking to his car in the opposite direction. So far, as private eyes go, we suck," Jessica joked, then continued, "On a more serious note, I have to go get ready for a party I'm going to with Pua later this afternoon. It's at some rich guy's house in Kukio. I wish I could bring you along, but Pua said she was only allowed to bring a plus one."

"No worries, I have to call the client and let him know that we didn't get the photo today and see if he wants to try again next week."

2

———

Pua had made it to the pinnacle of the food chain in the Hawaii real estate business. Her social circle was the who's who of the Big Island.

Her biggest client, billionaire Hiroshi Tamashiro, invited her and a guest to a housewarming party to show off his new beach house at the Kukio Resort. Tamashiro built the most expensive home in the multimillion-dollar resort's history. According to an article in the Wall Street Journal the price tag exceeded forty million dollars.

For this party, Pua invited Jessica to come along, to be her wingman, since Sam and Henry were away on an overnight fishing trip.

She and Jessica arrived a little late to the party because they stopped at Costco and couldn't find the exact bottle of Dom Perignon she wanted to bring as a housewarming gift.

After wandering through the liquor isle for the third time, Jessica said, "It's for a man, remember? Get him something he can eat, and he'll be happy. Look over there at the bakery," as Jessica pointed to a big table of pastries. "How about a dozen blueberry muffins."

Pua shook her head and said, "Not happening." After

another five minutes of looking for just the right bottle, she picked up a vintage bottle of wine that cost twice as much as she had hoped to spend and said, "This will work."

Jessica's eyebrows rose when she glanced at the shelf where the bottle had been and saw the $800 price tag.

"You must really like this client. He's lucky it wasn't me buying the gift, or he'd be getting muffins," Jessica said as they got into Pua's Mercedes.

The sisters were getting along better than they ever had in the past, but they still had trying moments from time to time and Jessica sensed they were on the verge of one of them if she didn't quit needling Pua about the price of the wine.

After arriving at the party, Pua ordered a rum Mai Tai and Jessica iced tea. Pua didn't waste any time downing the drink, then grabbed another one from a waiter passing by with a tray of them.

After he was out of earshot, Pua said, "You wonder why I'm so materialistic, I'll tell you why. It goes back to the day my boyfriend left me with a baby, no food, no money and no job. I swore I'd never allow myself to be put in that position again."

A few minutes after she started on the second drink, the truth serum began to work its magic on her and she segued into, "I'm not even mad about it anymore, that was years ago. But, I'm over dating for love. From now on, it's all about the money. No money, no honey, is my simple rule to live by," she whispered into Jessica's ear as she stirred her drink. "Besides, love is highly overrated."

Jessica shook her head, "I'm sorry I wasn't here to help you back then, but I see a hard road ahead for you and–I'll be driving when we leave."

"We'll see about that," Pua scoffed.

They continued to mingle by the pool, taking in the view of the massive luau grounds with its exotic tropical landscape that surrounded the three-acre oceanfront estate. The borders of the property were lined with yellow hibiscus flowers. Red and green ti leaves had been strategically placed around the property at the direction of a Feng Shui expert brought in to supervise the building of the property. There was a mixture of plumeria trees planted throughout the grounds, all of them dripping with various colors of flowers: yellow, white, pink, and red.

"Speaking of boyfriends, how's that working out being in business with an ex?" Jessica asked.

"It's okay, Charles is good at managing the property rentals and I don't need to supervise him, so it works."

For the past few months, Pua had attended parties at Kukio and the Four Seasons Resort looking for Mr. Right, or Mr. Right Now, depending on her mood. These were the only places on the island where she could stalk potential billionaire boyfriends and prospect for high-end clients simultaneously.

As Pua scanned the throng of people gathered around the pool, she said to Jessica, "I lost out on one stray billionaire living up on a huge coffee estate in Holualoa. I had him at the top of my list for quite a while." She paused, took a sip of her drink and sighed before continuing. "I'd hoped he would be here tonight, but it wasn't meant to be, I guess. I found out from a friend this morning that a gold digger from California scooped him up while I wasn't paying attention. My source said, not long after that the hoochie momma convinced him they should pack the jet and move back to the mainland so she would be closer to her favorite mall."

Pua shook her head in disgust as she continued to scan the crowd. "My friend also said the woman looked like a worn-out Barbie with fake boobs and skin like an alligator, from years of lying in the sun."

"Why don't you try looking for a nice guy instead?" Jessica said.

"I am—a nice rich guy."

"I can see it annoys you to no end that big boobs Barbie swooped in and stole your man. Especially since you stalked him for a long time, and we both know you're the better catch. Besides, you're a triathlete, you've finished Ironman three times. And you're the president of your real estate company. Oh, and I almost forgot-you're definitely a nine on a scale of ten appearance wise," Jessica smirked.

Pua ignored the sarcasm and, in the spirit of getting along, pasted on a fake grin and nodded.

The fact that her sister met and fell in love with a billionaire without even trying, annoyed her. She could hook rich guys, but she just couldn't keep them on the line for more than a month at a time. Jessica started referring to Pua's boyfriends using the months of the year instead of their names.

Pua thought for sure Mr. December, as Jessica liked to call him, would be the one to become serious with. They made it a whole two months together, and that was a record for her after Charles. But that ended when Mr. December's wife showed up unexpectedly during the whirlwind romance.

She dated a few former clients briefly. Two of them also failed to disclose they were married, and while Pua wasn't interested in being the other woman, she did have champagne taste and wanted someone else to pay for it. A mink in the closet, a Jaguar in the garage, and a rich boyfriend to write the check, was her motto, but dating married men was a deal breaker.

Tired of the revolving door of men and approaching forty, it was clear to her the writing was on the wall. If she didn't land a rich husband soon, it would be too late.

Pua and Jessica continued to mingle as the evening wore on and Pua had switched to drinking iced tea, so she wouldn't make a fool of herself in front of her biggest client. Jessica admired Pua's ability to avert disaster when it came to alcohol; something she wasn't able to do back in her drinking days.

Finally, Mr. Tamashiro made his way over to their table and joined them for a few minutes. After Pua introduced him to Jessica, Mr. Tamashiro asked her to step away for a moment, so he could speak with her privately.

"Concerning the sale of the Holualoa property, I think Chablon is being unreasonable. I'm not willing to replace the roof. Tell him he can buy the property "as is" for the agreed upon price or the deal's off."

Pua nodded and Mr. Tamashiro left to continue greeting arriving party guests. Pua returned to the table and said to Jessica, "Are you ready to go? I have to go home and call Charles. My firm is representing Mr. Tamashiro and the buyer in the biggest deal of my career and it's not going to close if Charles and I don't get them on the same page." And she handed Jessica the keys to her Mercedes.

3

———————

I t was 7:45 a.m. and Charles Lim was the first to arrive at the oceanfront outdoor café. He took a seat at a corner table near the road, where a steady stream of vehicles passed by. It was a small two-person table with a perfect view of Kailua Bay.

Alii Drive in front of the restaurant was wet from the enormous surf spilling over it from the night before at high tide. The air was heavy with a salty mist blowing lightly toward Charles. He had become mesmerized watching the surfers ride large waves toward the rocky shoreline and dart away, at the last moment, almost as if they were playing chicken with the rocks.

At five feet five, a hundred and thirty-five pounds soaking wet, some of Charles' colleagues called him "mouse" because of his small stature and nervous disposition. He wore what some might consider the official men's real estate agent uniform in Kona: Tommy Bahama aloha shirt, board shorts, and flip-flops.

"Charles!" Pua Murphy thundered, as she heaved her keys down on top of the table.

Still focused on the surfers in the bay across the street, he hadn't noticed her walking toward him. After being jolted back to the present, he focused his attention on her and nervously picked up his coffee cup and took a sip as she sat down across from him.

She lowered her voice, "I'm sorry, I just got served a subpoena as I was leaving the office. Obviously, I'm still angry about it."

Charles' eyebrows furrowed, "Who's suing you?"

"You mean, who's suing us?"

Her eyes drilled into his before he could look away, and she continued, "One of our rental property owners. I have no idea why they've filed suit. I'll deal with it when I return to the office, but for now, we need to iron out a major problem before the close of escrow on the Tamashiro property. If we don't persuade Chablon to back off the demand for a new roof we're going to lose the sale."

Charles' face turned pale as if he had indigestion but he didn't say anything.

Not only were they in the biggest real estate deal of their lives, but they were also handling the whole transaction in house, which meant they didn't have to split their commission with another firm.

The selling price of the property was a shade over seventy million dollars, and Pua Murphy Real Estate had agreed to a three percent brokerage fee of just over two million at the close of sale.

"When this closes, we'll be set for life," Charles said, as he handed the coffee creamer across the table to Pua.

She was in no mood for Charles' overconfident attitude about it being a done deal.

"Don't count your money just yet. This sale is a long way from being closed, and I don't need you jinxing it," she snapped.

Pua had been selling real estate in Kona for a long time and knew better than to count the money before the sale closed. She had seen enough deals blow up at the closing table over the years for the stupidest things. The one sentence she hated to hear the most was, "It's not the money, it's the principle." Whenever anyone uttered those words, the deal was guaranteed to go up in smoke.

Cell phones all over the restaurant began to ping in rapid succession, one right after another, as people started pulling them out of their pockets and purses. It was the emergency warning from Hawaii Civil Defense. The message was ominous, "BALLISTIC MISSILE INBOUND TO HAWAII. SEEK IMMEDIATE SHELTER. THIS IS NOT A DRILL."

A nuclear missile striking Hawaii could kill them all.

Pua looked around the café, and people were calling loved ones in a panic, some were crying. A lot of them looked traumatized. She glanced back at Charles and his face had turned pale white again.

On the Big Island, there were no bomb shelters. And if the blast didn't kill you, the radiation fallout would.

Charles' hands shook, like an alcoholic that needed a drink, as he picked up his coffee cup. He quivered as he leaned forward over the table toward Pua and quietly said,

"I'm not going to die today full of guilt. I've got something I have to tell you in case you survive and I don't. I borrowed money out of the company rental property trust account. My plan was to pay it back when I got my commission from the sale of the Tamashiro property."

Pua's eyebrows narrowed and her teeth clenched together, "How much money have you 'borrowed'?"

Charles stared at the floor. He couldn't look her in the eye until he finally found the courage to answer. "About a hundred and fifty thousand."

Pua slammed her fist down on the table so hard it left a split down the middle and almost broke in half. People sitting nearby stared as she reached over the table and pointed her finger at Charles. "If the missile doesn't kill you, I swear I'll do it myself you son of a bitch."

Everybody in the place heard her say it–everybody.

She picked up her coffee mug, took a sip, and turned her chair toward Kailua Bay. She took a deep breath of the salt air through her nose, exhaled out her mouth and stared at the ocean waiting for the missile to hit. Her son, Kainoa, had gone fishing with Uncle Jack down at South Point where there wasn't any cell phone coverage, so she couldn't call and tell him she loved him one last time. The closest cell tower to her was jammed, and she couldn't get through to either of her sisters, Jessica or Jasmine. Twice she turned and glared at Charles, as she gnashed her teeth.

She thought if it were a false alarm, Civil Defense would've sent a retraction by now. She was sure the end would come any minute since news reports, in the week prior, said it would only take fifteen minutes for a missile to get to Hawaii from North Korea–twelve minutes had already passed.

Thirty-eight minutes later and the nuclear bomb never arrived. The only thing that finally did show up was a text message from Civil Defense saying the inbound missile threat message was a mistake.

Pua turned her chair back toward Charles. He had sat there the entire time and not uttered a word.

"Anything else you need to tell me about?"

Her eyes bore into his before he could look away.

"And how about you tell me why you took the money?"

What little color that had come back to his face had drained out once again.

"There might be one more little problem," he answered, barely louder than a whisper.

Pua was sorry she asked and changed her mind, "You can tell me the rest later, I've had enough confession for one morning."

In disgust, she stood and threw ten bucks down on the placemat next to her coffee cup. She placed a business card under the money after she quickly scribbled a note on the back of it that said to send her a bill for the table. She stormed out of the restaurant and went back to the office to think about what to do next. And how to prevent the financial ruin coming her way because of Charles.

4

———

P ua excelled at making money in real estate, but she didn't like keeping track of it. She hated the accounting side of business and struggled for years to keep an eye on the financials. The lack of oversight was how Charles embezzled a hundred and fifty thousand dollars without getting caught.

She was too busy making money hand over fist, selling multimillion dollar oceanfront properties, to bother with keeping track of the trust account money.

Two years before, Pua and Charles met while going to chemotherapy. She had breast cancer. He had stage three melanoma. When both of their cancers went into remission, they knew they'd escaped death and received second chances at life; they wanted to make the best of life going forward. They had a connection to each other similar to survivors of a shipwreck and were grateful to be alive.

At the time, Charles struggled to pay the bills as a musician while playing local nightclubs to put food on the table.

Pua encouraged him to go into real estate and, after getting his sales license, she asked him to move in with her and manage the rental property division of her company.

Initially, he was so good at running the property management business, she made him a junior partner after the second month.

Their romance bloomed, and they were in heaven, until about three months later when they realized they weren't the least bit compatible. He was an Atheist; she a Christian. He was pro-choice; she pro-life. He was a Democrat; she a Republican.

They fought over everything. They just didn't like each other much after the pink cloud of surviving cancer had worn off.

When the romance ended, Charles moved out after three and a half months. But Pua kept him on running the property management side of her business because he always seemed to have things running smoothly. And because she didn't have to run around getting plumbers all the time to fix stopped up toilets, she made more money. She also didn't have time to deal with getting rid of that part of her business, and him, at the same time even if she wanted to. Plus, he'd brought in a couple of big clients to the sales side of the brokerage, and sold a few high-end properties, besides managing the rentals.

Before he moved, Pua's neighbors in the condo complex across the street, called the cops on numerous occasions because of the loud arguments coming from Pua's house. Friends of the couple couldn't believe they lasted as long as they had. No charges were ever filed, and nobody ever got hauled off to jail. They never physically fought, Pua would have beat the hell out of Charles. Pua's friends didn't worry about Charles assaulting her. They all feared she would be the one arrested for battery since she held a brown belt in Kempo karate.

Pua's home and office were on Walua Road in the commercial district. The building wasn't anything fancy, it was just a simple plantation style with her real estate business downstairs and her living quarters upstairs.

A few minutes after arriving home, Pua got out a can of cat food for Molly, a grumpy Siamese with only one mood– bad. As she stroked the kitty, she thought about what Charles told her earlier that morning. She was jolted from her thoughts when a loud banging started on the side of the house at the top of the staircase. See looked out the living room window next to the stairs and saw a man she didn't recognize. Instead of going to the door, she slid the window open and said, "Can I help you?"

"I'm with the census and I sent you a survey that needs to be filled out and we never received a response."

She listened to the man go on and on for five minutes before cutting him off and said,

"I got the thing in the mail two days ago. I'll send the damn thing back when I have time to fill it out."

She slammed the window shut and flopped down on the couch below and sighed. A few minutes after the man left, she thought about her response, and regretted how she talked to him, but her emotions once again got the better of her.

"Oh well, I am sure he'll bring the FBI next time," she thought to herself.

A knock at the front door a few minutes later jolted Pua out of thought again. This time without looking out the window she went to the door and flung it open, ready to give that census taker both barrels, but saw Charles standing there instead.

"There's one more thing I have to tell you," he said as his eyes darted away from hers.

She didn't want to see him yet but relented because she needed to know everything he had done. She stood there with both arms crossed over her chest while breathing deeply trying to get control of her anger.

"Okay, what else have you done?"

His eyes turned toward Larry Black Realty next door, "I stole one of Larry's clients."

"Which client?" she demanded.

"Andre Chablon," he answered, his voice barely loud enough for Pua to hear.

It took every ounce of resolve for her not to kick Charles down the stairs. She glared at him but didn't say a word as she felt the rage boiling up inside. Charles couldn't stand the silence and blurted out, "Larry will never know I poached his client."

"You must be a special kind of stupid if you don't think he'll find out. You don't need to worry about him, I'm going to kill you myself," she screamed.

Sue Carter and Lillian Pelekane, two real estate agents who worked next door at Larry Black Realty, stood slack-jawed in the parking lot and watched as Pua threatened Charles.

Charles was many things, but stupid was not one of them. He didn't waste any time leaving and hurried down the stairs before Pua made good on her threat. In his haste to leave he almost ran straight into Jessica. She was there to pick up Pua, and had started up the stairs and got to the third step but stopped when she heard Pua yell at Charles.

Pua waved at Jessica to come on up. "Don't ask," as she held the screen door open for her sister.

"I'm almost ready, give me a few minutes," Pua said.

Jessica nodded and while Pua was inside she stayed out on the lanai and scanned the ocean activity going on down the hill from Pua's house. Most days a pod of dolphins cruised by every morning and Jessica timed it just right that morning and spotted them frolicking out front of the house.

Pua and Jessica went to the orchid show at the Old Airport Pavilion. Pua was so worked up, over what Charles told her earlier, she and Jessica barely talked about the nuclear missile false alarm, or anything else for that matter.

After the sisters each bought a couple of orchids, they walked across the Old Airport runway to the beach. They sat on a picnic table, next to a tall palm tree, close to the small waves that lapped the shoreline.

There was no breeze, it was eighty-nine degrees, and the humidity was thick enough to cut with a knife.

For the first three or four minutes the sisters gazed at the surfers riding waves before Pua said, "I'm screwed," as she stared straight ahead at the turquoise blue water. "Charles embezzled a hundred and fifty thousand dollars from my client's trust account. I will lose everything I've worked for and my real estate license, if I don't come up with the money to replace it."

Jessica put her arm around Pua's shoulder and gave her a light squeeze and joked, "You want me to kill him for you?"

"No, I'll do it myself," Pua replied, half joking. Tomorrow will be the day I find out if I'm out of business or not. The Tamashiro/Chablon deal is scheduled to close. If it closes, I'm okay. If it doesn't, I'm ruined."

5

Pua had one last chance to get Mr. Tamashiro and Andre Chablon to agree to the terms of the sale of Tamashiro's coffee estate in Holualoa. The parties all agreed to meet that morning at her office to try to close the deal.

The sticking point in the sale was that during the property inspection, it was found that the roof of the main house needed substantial repair. Chablon wanted a major price reduction or else he was going to walk, but Mr. Tamashiro wasn't having any part of lowering the price.

Tamashiro didn't care if the property sold or not, and was firm that, if it did, it would sell as is at the price he listed it for. And the price that Chablon originally agreed to.

The largest real estate deal in island history was heading toward the rocks, but Pua wanted to try one last idea to salvage it by offering to pay for the cost of the roof replacement out of her commission just to close the transaction.

By that point, both buyer and seller hated each other and neither of them would agree to Pua's offer since they appeared to be having a contest to see who could be the most stubborn.

But when Chablon uttered those three dreaded words Pua hated hearing the most, that sealed the death of the deal.

"It's the principle," Mr. Chablon said, as he turned and walked out the door.

After Tamashiro and Chablon left her office, Pua sat at her desk, in absolute despair, knowing that she was financially ruined without that commission.

6

The next morning, Pua went for a five-mile run down Alii Drive. The thing she liked about running along the coast was the view of the ocean and the salty air helped clear her head. The time alone allowed her to think about how she would deal with the bombshell revelations Charles told her the day before. And how she would come up with the money to cover the missing property deposits. As far as poaching Larry Black's client went, she prayed he would never find out. That was the conclusion she came to after she ran about three miles.

Returning from her run, she jogged up the driveway and saw Charles' car in the parking lot behind her office building. She hoped he was in the office clearing out his desk. Because if he wasn't, she'd do it for him after she got out of the shower, and it wouldn't be pretty. She sprinted past the office door and up the stairs, to her quarters, so she could get ready for work.

While in the shower, as she washed her hair, she heard a loud commotion downstairs in the office. She couldn't tell who was doing the yelling. She heard another loud noise through the floor; it wasn't people arguing, it sounded like furniture being knocked over, but the noise stopped as quickly as it started.

Probably just another angry renter who hadn't received their deposit back after moving out, having left the place destroyed. She loathed the rental business but took it on, during the Great Recession, so she could keep the doors open when nothing was selling.

Pua got out of the shower, slipped on an aloha print sundress and towel dried her hair. After a quick touch of lip gloss, she checked herself in the mirror before heading downstairs to the office.

When she opened the door, she stopped-frozen at the sight of Charles, who lay prone on the floor, next to his desk, in a pool of blood coming from a large gash on the right side of his forehead. A bloody shark's tooth club appeared to be the murder weapon, and lay beside his skull.

Pua called 911 and told the operator she had just arrived at work and found Charles bludgeoned. She didn't cry or yell; she was in shock; her world was crumbling all around her. After she got off the phone, she thought about who would do this to him? Larry Black? A disgruntled renter? There were plenty of people who didn't like Charles. But murder him over it? These were the thoughts that raced through her mind as she waited for the police to show up. Larry Black had about a million dollars' worth of reason to want Charles dead. That thought kept pushing the others out of her head.

Police vehicles swarmed the parking lot of Pua Murphy Real Estate within minutes of her 911 call. She sat on the stairs outside the office while she waited. When the first officer on the scene got out of his SUV and approached Pua, she pointed toward the office door. She didn't move, but continued to dial Jessica, over and over; she needed her sister more than ever.

7

By the time the medical examiner arrived at Pua Murphy Real Estate, there was an audience in the parking lot next door at Larry Black Realty. Small clusters of real estate agents huddled together, whispering to each other about what might have happened. Among them were Sue Carter and Lillian Pelekane. Lillian was a cousin of Detective Kaipo, who just pulled into the lot behind Pua's building. She waved and motioned to him to come over and talk before he entered the crime scene. She was almost giddy as she told him the details of how she and Sue Carter heard Pua threaten to kill Charles the day before.

"Did anyone else witness the threat being made?" Detective Kaipo asked.

"Her sister, Jessica Kealoha," Sue Carter replied and added, "Her husband, Sam Stewart, does a lot of business with our boss, Larry Black, that's how I know her name." Lillian nodded.

Kaipo jotted down a quick note, thanked her and Lillian then went to check out the murder scene.

Detective Kaipo had been with the Kona PD for twenty-two years and during that time he probably investigated maybe a dozen murders. This case didn't appear any different from the others he'd worked. Kona averaged about one murder a year, sometimes two. This one looked like all the rest. Someone got mad, and someone got hit in the head with a weapon, and now they're dead.

The crime scene photographer finished taking photos of Charles sprawled out on the floor beside his desk. Paul Holwick, the medical examiner, stood next to Charles' body.

"Howzit Paul?" Kaipo asked.

"Good," he answered, while he focused on his clipboard as he wrote notes.

Detective Kaipo knelt to take a closer look, to inspect the gash on Charles' head. "What do you think, Paul?"

"I think the guy forgot to duck."

Officer Powell, who was the first responder on the scene, stuck his head in the doorway and interrupted Kaipo and Holwick.

"Pua Murphy found the body, she's sitting out here on the stairs when you're ready to talk to her Detective." Kaipo nodded.

Pua sat on the stairs the entire time, trying to reach Jessica, as the police investigated the crime scene.

After Detective Kaipo finished talking with the medical examiner, he stepped outside to speak with Pua. "Could you come down to the station and make a statement?" he asked.

"Sure, but let me try calling my sister one more time before we go."

And once again she got Jessica's voice mail, so she left a message saying she was going to the police station with Detective Kaipo to give a statement.

The interview room at the station had a small table and two chairs. After Pua and Detective Kaipo sat down, he asked her, "Would you like something to drink? We have coffee, tea, soda, or water."

"No thanks."

Just the thought of drinking something made Pua feel even more nauseous than she already was since finding Charles' body.

Pua was like most people who weren't criminal lawyers. She didn't see any harm in talking to the police and thought by doing so it might help them find the killer and clear up any ideas they might have that she murdered Charles.

Detective Kaipo didn't waste any time getting to the point. "We found prints on the murder weapon, are we going to find out they match yours?"

Pua leaned forward in her chair, tapped the index finger of her right hand on the table and looked Kaipo straight in the eye as she said, "If I wanted to kill him, I wouldn't need a club."

Before she could say another word, Jessica barged into the interview room. Detective Kaipo, visibly annoyed, glared at her and in an authoritative tone of voice said, "We're busy here."

"Is she under arrest?" Jessica questioned, as she returned the same tone.

"No, are you her attorney?"

Jessica ignored the question as she grabbed Pua's shoulder with a firm grip and coaxed her up out of the chair.

"We're out of here. She's not talking to you any further without a lawyer."

Since he had nothing to hold her on, Detective Kaipo didn't respond as he watched Jessica quickly lead Pua out of the interview room.

Captain Sid Akiona was on the phone in his office, talking to Chief Matsumoto in Hilo when he noticed a familiar woman on the security monitor and realized it was Jessica. When he finished his call with the chief, he came out to the waiting area to see her, but all he found was Detective Kaipo standing there staring at Pua and Jessica, through the glass exit door, as they walked across the parking lot.

Kaipo glanced at Sid, "You look like you lost your puppy?"

"Funny, I was about to say the same thing to you-the one on the right used to be my partner years ago."

After Jessica and Pua walked out the front door of the station, Pua said, "I was just trying to be helpful and didn't think there was any harm in talking to Detective Kaipo."

"Don't say anything else until we're in the car," Jessica said.

Before Jessica retired from the LAPD, she had arrested lots of people over the years that came down to the station for an interview. She knew how the game worked and didn't want her sister to become a victim of the system.

After they got in her car, Jessica rolled up the windows to make sure their conversation remained private. She didn't mince words, "Listen, if you want to stay out of prison, you will never talk to that detective again without a lawyer present, understand?"

Like a somber child, Pua nodded in agreement.

"And speaking of lawyers, I'm going to contact one as soon as we get to your house."

"Dad's old attorney, Jamison?" Pua asked.

"Oh, hell no! You'll go to prison for sure if that hack represents you. I know who to call."

8

———

Before Jessica called a lawyer for Pua, the first thing she did was call Gabbie.

Gabbie picked up right away because she was just getting ready to call Jessica.

"What's up?" Gabbie answered.

"We're done trying to get a photo of Charles and Erica," Jessica said.

"How did you know Larry didn't want us to pursue it anymore?" Gabbie asked.

"I didn't, but Charles is dead, somebody clubbed him in the head at Pua's office. So I'm going to bow out of taking any more cases until I know Pua is in the clear on this, since they had a history. If they charge her, I'm going to have to devote all my time to helping her," Jessica said.

"If you need my help, just let me know," Gabbie replied and Jessica hung up the phone.

Jessica's next call was to Lori Makani, attorney at law, and she gave her all the details of Charles Lim's murder.

Lori was a high-profile criminal defense lawyer on Oahu and lifelong friend of Jessica's. If a mobster was charged with murder in the state of Hawaii, Lori was who they called.

The yakuza made up most of her business over the years. Almost all of them were dead or in prison now. She had been a lawyer for the Japanese mob for a long time and as a result, well paid over the years. Besides the money, she never worried about any of her other thug clients giving her trouble because it was common knowledge around town the mob protected her.

Jessica didn't care about any of that. All she cared about was Pua not going to prison, and Lori was her sister's best chance of not getting convicted and locked up for life.

Lori sat at her desk in the corner office on the twenty-fourth floor across the street from Aloha Tower in Honolulu, waiting for Jessica and Pua to arrive. She stared out the window at Pearl Harbor, watching a Navy destroyer leave the harbor. Her secretary's voice crackled over the intercom, "Your two o'clock is here."

"Show them in."

A few years had passed since she had last seen Jessica. For Pua, it was at least twenty years. When they entered the office, she hugged them both like long-lost family.

Jessica normally didn't have any love for criminal defense lawyers, but Lori was different. They grew up together on the Big Island, and they survived a serial killer who targeted them when they were twenty years old. They had a special bond having escaped the harrowing event together.

Hawaiian motif decorated the office, complete with Lori's canoe paddle on the wall and a painting of Queen Lili-uokalani. She made the office as comfortable as possible since she practically lived there most days of the week.

Lori invited Pua and Jessica to the long black leather couch positioned against the wall, underneath the paddle and the painting of the Queen. Lori sat in the plump leather chair catty corner to the couch.

The decor looked more like something you would see in a psychiatrist's office than an attorney's.

"I don't think they have an open and shut case," Lori stated.

Pua sighed a breath of relief, Jessica just focused on Lori's eyes.

"But, you have some problems. One is Detective Kaipo. He wants to close the case and retire as soon as possible. That is according to one of my sources inside the Kona PD. And pinning this on the first available suspect is what he'll likely want to do, and that suspect would be you. My source also said a lot of people heard you twice threaten to kill Charles." Lori turned her eyes to Jessica, "And they have a witness that said you were there when she threatened him, so if this goes to trial, expect to be called by the prosecution."

Jessica sighed and looked out the window toward the harbor for a minute while shaking her head.

Lori took a piece of nicotine gum from her purse before sitting down. She put it in her mouth and continued.

"I've done some checking and another problem is Governor Fitch. Charles Lim was his nephew, and he wants somebody's ass in jail for murdering him. My source at HPD says that Fitch has pulled strings and sent one of the best detectives in the Honolulu PD to Kona to help Kaipo get the case closed; his name is Swanson. In the last year, he's closed more cases than any other detective in Honolulu. A couple former clients, that he's arrested, swear he planted evidence in their cases. So if he thinks you're guilty, he'll do whatever it takes to convict you."

Pua had moved up to the edge of the sofa and listened intently when Lori started talking about the problems facing her. She flung herself back into the thick, padded pillows of the couch and took a deep breath in through her nose and slowly exhaled from her mouth.

Looking perplexed, Pua said, "I didn't know the governor was Charles' uncle, he never mentioned it."

Lori continued, "I think Kaipo and Swanson will build a

case against you and submit it to the Hawaii County prosecutor who then will decide whether to charge you with murder."

Pua sprung back up straight with her arms up in the air, "I didn't murder Charles!"

"That's irrelevant to me, my job is to keep you out of prison and that's what I plan to do," Lori said.

Jessica raised an eyebrow, but said nothing.

Up to this point Pua had been rather subdued when it came to Charles' murder and Jessica wasn't quite sure if she was innocent-until now. She knew from experience that people who weren't guilty almost always got louder and louder when it came to saying they didn't do the crime. While Lori said she didn't care if Pua did it, Jessica certainly did.

Before Pua and Jessica left the meeting, Lori looked at Pua and said, "A couple of things before you go. If they arrest you, I'll be on the next flight to Kona for the arraignment. And do not say anything to them other than 'I want my lawyer.' No idle chit-chat, nothing. Anything you say can be used against you, no matter how innocent you might think the words are. They can pick sound bites out of what you tell them and use it in court and the next thing you know you're doing life in prison. Keep your mouth shut. Understand?"

Pua nodded. Jessica and Pua thanked Lori for her time and left for the airport to return to Kona.

Jessica texted Sam that they were on the way back to the plane but got no answer. Twenty minutes later, the taxi dropped them off at the Honolulu airport. While Jessica and Pua met with Lori, Sam went to see his doctor at Moanalua Hospital. He was experiencing a lot of pain from a failed back surgery earlier in the year and wanted the doctor to prescribe something stronger, which he did. When Jessica and Pua returned to the plane Sam was there; he was reclined in his seat, knocked out from the new more powerful pain killer the doctor prescribed.

Jessica had noticed in the past few weeks that he ate pain pills like Chiclets gum, and it concerned her that it looked like he was becoming addicted to them.

As the Gulfstream jet climbed out of Honolulu, on the way back to Kona, Jessica peered out the window as they passed over Diamond Head. She thought about how hard her struggle to beat addiction was and that she was powerless to help him if in fact he was becoming addicted to his medication. But now she didn't have time to think about Sam possibly being addicted, she needed to start an investigation, so she could keep Pua from going to prison for the rest of her life.

9

Before Charles' graveside service, those who attended looked more like they were at a Chamber of Commerce mixer. A dozen real estate agents showed up to pay their last respects. Sam and Jessica came to support Pua since she had been ostracized by almost everyone in town, including her colleagues in the real estate industry.

Larry Black tried to ignore his wife Erica as he quietly chatted with other real estate brokers before the service started, while she worked to anger him by flirting with a good-looking man at least twenty years her junior. Flirting with younger men, in front of Larry, was something Erica liked to do just to make him jealous. But to flaunt it publicly was a different matter altogether. After they left the funeral, there would be a price to pay. It was no secret he had slapped her around in the past and this day wouldn't be any different in the end. The irony was Erica would sometimes stay in the women's shelter that she and Larry's foundation funded every year. After a few days, she'd go back home to him, and he'd promise to never do it again, and they'd have make up sex and the cycle would start all over.

The real circus took place after the funeral. Charles'

memorial was being held at the Ocean View Restaurant across from the Kailua pier; Governor Fitch rented the entire restaurant. It was a large open air room with a view of the pier and Kailua Bay.

Every starving real estate agent in Kona made an appearance that day since there would be an enormous amount of free food. Most of them who tried to appear successful, did so by driving old Mercedes, but didn't have two nickels to rub together on any given day of the week. Anytime the opportunity for a free meal arose, they showed up en masse. Half of them probably didn't even know Charles.

Pua watched clusters of agents, seated together around the room, whisper and look in her direction as she sat with Sam and Jessica at a table in the center of the dining room that overlooked the ocean. It looked a lot like the time a white tip reef shark had circled Pua while she snorkeled alone off Magic Sands Beach. Getting out of the water at the time was the smart thing to do. Now the sharks, of the two-legged variety, were circling, and she was just going to have to sit there and watch them for the time being.

Larry Black arrived at the memorial alone, strolled through the crowded room looking for a place to sit and asked Sam and Jessica if he might join them at their table with Pua. Pua's face turned pale like she had seen a ghost but she said nothing.

"Of course, sit down." Sam motioned Larry toward the other side of the booth where Pua was sitting. Larry slid into the half-moon booth opposite of Sam and Jessica. To make room, Pua slid as close as possible next to Jessica, as if recoiling from a hot flame.

Larry and Pua's offices shared a common driveway, but the two of them hadn't spoken in over a year. Larry had tried a couple of times, but Pua always kept from making eye contact and hurried into her office whenever Larry was in the parking lot or driveway. She didn't need any drama with Erica accusing her of trying to steal her man again, like the time years earlier at the gentlemen's club they both worked at in Honolulu.

Sam's company was building a super yacht to spec for a Russian oligarch represented by Larry's Yacht Brokerage firm. Larry's core business was real estate, but yacht sales and exotic cars were his secondary business. His mission was to handle all the needs of his uber-wealthy clientele that he specialized in. Larry Black operated a one stop shop as he liked to call it. His average client spent ten million dollars with him if they bought one each of what he was selling. He sold estates, yachts, and cars all under one roof. People swore Larry could sell ice to an Eskimo.

During that time, Sam and Jessica were acquainted with him well enough to not ask many questions. Not that they feared he would hurt them, but the less they knew about him the better, in case he was ever indicted for money laundering-or worse.

Sam and Larry met many times over the previous year to discuss the progress of the oligarch's yacht and to talk about design changes the client wanted. Sam normally didn't work in the day to day running of the yacht building business anymore, but this particular boat was the most expensive one his company ever contracted for and the first one ever sold to a Russian oligarch, so he personally oversaw all aspects of the production.

An oligarch had many rich friends who would likely buy more yachts from Sam's company, so he wanted to make sure everything was perfect.

"Where's Erica?" Sam asked.

"She didn't feel well, so I dropped her off at home," Larry answered.

A few minutes later, the waiter appeared and asked everyone what they would like to drink.

"I'll have Vodka," Larry said. Pua followed with a shot of tequila, and Sam and Jessica settled on iced tea.

When the drinks came, Sam swallowed a pain pill with his tea. It was the third time Jessica saw him take one that day and it was clear a showdown was coming soon over the excessive number of pills he was taking every day.

A local newspaper reporter for Hawaii Island News, Amanda Lee, walked up to the table and greeted everyone.

"Pua, I'm writing an article, it would be great if you would call me tomorrow, so I can get your side of the story before it goes to press." She leaned over the table and set her business card down in front of Pua, smiled at everyone and left to mingle with the crowd.

"I got to run too," Larry said, just before gulping down the last of his drink.

Sam's pain pill kicked in, and he nodded off. Jessica shot him a look and then turned back to Pua, "What do you think Amanda Lee is working on that she wants to talk to you about?"

"Nothing good, it's all nothing good," Pua answered, as she downed another shot of tequila.

10

After Lillian Pelekane's statement saying she heard Pua threaten Charles, and reviewing reports indicating Kona patrol responded to Pua's home to investigate multiple loud arguments reported by neighbors, Detectives Kaipo and Swanson, who were now working together on the case, liked Pua a lot for the murder of Charles Lim.

Based on her volatile relationship with him, according to the neighbors, and the fact multiple witnesses said they heard her threaten his life, she now sat at the top of their list of possible suspects.

The big problem for the detectives, they didn't have a motive. It went away when the front-page article about Pua's business appeared in the local newspaper. The headline read that Charles Lim of Pua Murphy Real Estate embezzled $150,000 from forty-seven rental property owners.

After further investigation by police, they determined Charles alone took the deposit money. But since they couldn't prosecute him due to his demise, there would be no further involvement on their part concerning the embezzlement. They told the victims they would have to sue Pua Murphy Real Estate for the return of their deposits. And that's exactly what they did. All forty-seven of them, since the police said the missing money no longer constituted a theft, but a civil matter, and the chief suspect was no longer available to arrest.

After Kaipo and Swanson learned Charles stole the rental deposits, they could show Pua's motive. A week later they sent the case to the county prosecutor's office, who then assigned it to Deputy District Attorney Carrie King. She had a reputation as a tough prosecutor and was not afraid to bend the rules to get a conviction.

Six months after Charles' death people around town still acted like it happened the week before. Pua couldn't go anywhere in town without them glaring at her. Even though Charles stole the rental deposits, people hated the idea she killed him and there still weren't any charges filed in the case against her.

With all the negative press about Pua's company being blamed for the thousands of dollars missing from the rental property trust, people wanted blood–Pua's blood. There was a string of letters to the editor in the local paper weekly asking why Pua Murphy wasn't in jail for either Charles' murder or the theft of the rental property deposits. People didn't care much that Charles ripped off the money, it was Pua's company, and they wanted her to pay both the money back and serve time in jail. And a murder charge was the icing on the cake.

Pua returned home after a morning swim at the pier. As she walked up the driveway, she spotted a good-looking, well-dressed man leaning against his car, in the parking lot behind her office. She guessed him to be about six two,

two hundred twenty pounds. He didn't appear to be a real estate agent to her. In Kona, they all dressed like they were going to a luau instead of work. He looked familiar, but she couldn't place him.

He wore tan slacks with an aloha shirt neatly tucked in. There was something on his belt to the side, but she couldn't quite tell what it was from the angle he leaned against his car.

Since he appeared to be waiting, it was apparent he read the sign on the office door. It said Pua Murphy would be in by 9 a.m. When she noticed him, her first thought was *hmm, a potential client first thing in the morning. What a great way to start the day. Or another process server, ugh.*

"Aloha, I'm Pua Murphy, how can I help you?" she said, as she approached him.

The man smiled as he moved away from the car toward her.

"Pua Murphy, I have a warrant for your arrest," he said, as he reached behind his back and pulled out a pair of handcuffs from the small leather case attached to his belt. His badge, clipped to his belt over his hip, was now clearly visible as he stood facing squarely toward her.

Pua had settled into a false sense of security over the past few months and didn't think she'd be charged with Charles' murder. As Detective Swanson squeezed the handcuffs tight against her wrists, reality began to set in, as a pang in her gut that wouldn't go away anytime soon.

The only thing she could do was put on a brave face.

"Where's Kaipo, I figured he would be the one putting the cuffs on me if I got arrested?"

"He retired a couple months ago."

Swanson proceeded to read Pua her rights as a small cluster of agents gathered at the window of Larry Black Realty next door and gawked, as she stood there handcuffed.

Erica Black drove up the driveway that separated the two

real estate companies, in her black Mercedes-Benz, just in time to see Pua be handcuffed.

Just before the detective put Pua in the back of his unmarked Crown Vic, Erica parked and got out of her car. She slowly walked across the parking lot to her office before she turned and looked at Pua in the back seat of the detective's car.

Erica stared just long enough for Pua to notice, then smirked before she looked away, as she continued on to the office. The look of satisfaction on Erica's face caused the sharp pain in Pua's gut to be replaced with anger. She and Erica were once friends and co-workers at a private men's club in Honolulu, and parted company after Erica's wealthy boyfriend dumped her and started dating Pua a week later. From that time on they were enemies and acted as if the other didn't exist.

L ori Makani was on the next flight to Kona to appear at Pua's arraignment and argue for a reduction in bail. It was clear Deputy DA Carrie King had it in for Pua when she asked for one million dollars in bail.

Before the arraignment, Lori met Pua at the Kona cellblock to talk about the case before going to the courthouse.

Lori's tone was dead serious when she said, "Carrie King is the prosecutor. That woman is ruthless and won't let the truth get in the way of convicting you, it's all about winning for her. I've been up against her in Honolulu before she moved over here."

"I know about her," Pua admitted, as she thought about spending the rest of her life in prison and tried to ignore that wrenching feeling in her gut that returned in full force at the mention of Carrie King's name.

"How do you know her?" Lori asked.

"Back when I lived on the North Shore, my boyfriend at

the time belonged to the yakuza. The cops arrested him for murder, and they thought I might have been involved too. The only crime I committed was I just happened to have the wrong boyfriend back then."

"What was his name?" Lori asked.

"Kazumi Yoshimura," Pua answered.

Lori took in a deep breath and held it for a moment before letting it out, as she tapped a finger on the desk between her and Pua.

"I remember him. I was fresh out of law school back then, and if I recall correctly, his lawyer made an egregious mistake at trial and it got Yoshimura locked up for life. That, and the fact that he did the murder. How did I not know you were his girlfriend? Your name wasn't in the newspapers or anything."

"My grandfather made a deal with the District Attorney, Carrie King's boss, who was running for re-election at the time, to keep my name out of the investigation. Apparently, my grandfather had some dirt on the DA that he threatened to make public as leverage."

"That makes sense. It wasn't long after that your grandfather hired me for the first time to work on a case."

Later that morning Lori argued at the preliminary hearing that the bail amount was outrageous, and the judge agreed and reduced it to $250,000. A trial date was set and Pua was released later that day after Jessica posted her bond.

Pua had only been home a few minutes when there was a loud knock on the security door at the top of the staircase of her home. She discreetly peered through the window to see who it was. A man with flowers stood there looking around waiting for someone to come to the door. He was holding a beautiful bouquet of red roses.

I wonder who they're from. Maybe Detective Swanson wants to make up for arresting me? she kidded herself, as she walked to the door to open it.

"Pua Murphy?"

"Yes."

The man started to hand the flowers to her but instead reached inside the middle of the bouquet and pulled out a summons and slipped it to her instead as she started to reach for the flowers.

"You've been served," he said, as he turned and jogged down the stairs. Pua stood there reading the summons; another one of many more to come.

"Hey–don't I get the flowers, too?" she yelled as he left.

11

―――――

Pua being charged in Charles' murder brought back memories that Jessica hadn't thought about in over twenty years, back when she herself was facing a manslaughter charge before she became a cop. She was aware of how it felt to be investigated for murder by the police. Her gut ached just thinking about it. She needed to find out who killed Charles, or Pua was going away for life.

Jessica went to the Kailua Pier three days a week to swim the two-mile-long triathlon course. A mile out and a mile back was invigorating. Being back on the island a couple of years, since she retired from the LAPD, it was wonderful to get back in the ocean regularly. Sometimes after she swam she would have coffee, while she sat on the seawall and talked story with Freddie, a homeless man who was a familiar face in the village. Freddie had become an icon over the years.

He had a slim build with weather-beaten, tanned skin that looked like leather and long, blondish gray dreadlocks. Nobody remembered how long he had been in town, but most old-timers would agree it was well over thirty years. Unlike a lot of the homeless who kept to themselves, Freddie was sociable and could be seen almost every day having coffee, as he talked story with a variety of folks at Lava Java's outdoor patio, on Alii Drive across from Kailua Bay.

Over twenty years before, Jessica's partner on the Kona PD, Sid Akiona, introduced her to Freddie when she was a rookie cop. Freddie watched everything that went on in the village; he knew who all the drug dealers were, all the good cops, all the not so good ones, and all the other assorted riffraff. Freddie knew everybody–and everybody knew Freddie.

Jessica showed him a picture of Charles and asked if he had ever seen him before? He said he had; he'd seen Charles buy dope a few times in the village from a drug dealer named Bumpy.

"Do you know Bumpy's last name?" Jessica asked.

Freddie shook his head.

"Anything else you remember about the man in the photo?"

Freddie took a sip of his coffee and nodded.

"Yeah, he didn't look the part. I've known a lot of dope fiends over the years, and this guy didn't fit the profile. He was way too clean cut looking. And a couple of times I saw him make buys, he got out of a big black Mercedes that a woman was driving."

Jessica thanked Freddie and slipped him a twenty-dollar bill, then left in search Bumpy.

J essica found Bumpy at Emma's Square in the village, just like Freddie said she would. He was sitting on a bench across from the tree in the center of the square, waiting for the next customer. He fit the description Freddie had given her; local, about fifty, and covered in jail tattoos.

"Howzit," Jessica said, as she approached Bumpy.

Bumpy nodded but said nothing. She could tell he was sizing her up.

"Was this guy a regular customer?" she asked, as she flashed him a picture of Charles.

Bumpy ignored her and looked away.

"I just need to know and that will be the end of our conversation. If not, you can expect Vice to be down here to put an end to your little entrepreneurial endeavor."

Bumpy turned back toward Jessica, "Yeah, I know-um, he was a regular kine customer," he answered with a thick pidgin accent.

Jessica nodded and walked away when Bumpy said, "We good sista?" She didn't look back and kept on walking toward the public parking lot to get in her car. "Eh!" Bumpy yelled as he followed her to the lot above Emma's Square.

Jessica turned and faced him. "No, you piece of crap, we're not good. You sell poison that kills people. Your people. I'm going to keep my end of the bargain and leave you to do your thing. But if I ever have the chance later to make sure they lock your ass up, you can rest assured I'll do my best to see to it."

Bumpy backed down and made a quick retreat back to his bench at Emma's Square. It was the smartest thing he'd done that day.

After Jessica got in her car, she glanced at her phone and saw she had a half dozen missed calls from Uncle Jack and Pua.

The first call she returned was to Pua and it went straight to voice mail. She left a quick message, "I found out where the hundred and fifty grand went. Charles was a heroin addict."

12

———

Jessica listened to the message twice that said Sam was in the emergency room at the Kona hospital, to make sure she understood correctly. That morning she drove her dad's '69 Roadrunner to the pier. As she left the parking lot, she battled the urge to race 140 mph up the highway to the hospital. She settled on 90 and pulled into the emergency room parking lot seven minutes later.

When she arrived, she found Uncle Jack at the front entrance waiting for her. He was in the neighborhood and happened to stop by their house to see Sam just as the paramedics arrived.

"The gardener found Sam slumped over in a chair on the lanai and called 911," Uncle Jack said.

Jessica's eyes were red-rimmed and watery as she listened to him, and she stuffed her emotions to keep from crying. The thought of losing Sam made her gut ache unlike anything she ever felt before in her life.

Uncle Jack hugged her and continued, "The paramedics found a bottle of hydrocodone sitting next to him on the table and administered naloxone to save his life. He's going to be okay."

Jessica nodded and wiped the tears away before she and Uncle Jack went inside to talk to the ER doctor.

"I want to keep him overnight, and then he needs to go to rehab," Dr. Chay told them.

Sam's use of pain pills concerned Jessica for a few months before he overdosed and now, he was officially a drug addict. She would do whatever she needed to do to help him get clean. But she was aware of the fact she couldn't fix him, and he would need to do that part on his own.

She sat by the bed all night, holding Sam's hand while he slept. She vacillated between thoughts of how she would help him, and Pua, both simultaneously. A feeling of being overwhelmed engulfed her. Then a thought entered her mind; you're really not that powerful, you know. Sam will have to save Sam. And just like that it became clear to her she would put Sam in God's hands and do the footwork to save Pua. Most of her life she leaned toward being agnostic and still thought the jury was out when it came to whether or not God existed. But Sam believed there was, so she thought why not? She recognized the odds facing him were steep, and he needed all the help he could get, but she also believed he had the strength to get clean. But staying clean would be the hard part. And what if he couldn't?

Jessica went home to search the house. The thing about billionaires is the normal rules of life don't apply to them. Because of her previous battle with addiction, she knew of all the tricks an addict would most likely use to keep the supply of drugs flowing. There was an excellent chance Sam obtained multiple prescriptions for pain pills, from different doctors in different states, since he made regular visits to his various businesses all over the country. She would find the prescriptions she could and put all the doctors who wrote them on notice that if they ever wrote Sam another prescription, for anything stronger than penicillin, she would notify the DEA.

The first place in their house Jessica searched was the

study. After rummaging through Sam's desk she found three bottles of pills from doctors along the west coast; two of them in California and one in Seattle. Since Sam traveled in his own plane, getting more pills wasn't a problem-until now. After getting off the phone with all three doctors, she was ninety-nine percent sure he wouldn't be ordering any more pills from them.

A wall of French doors in the study led to the garden with a spectacular view of Keauhou Bay. Jessica spotted a hawk circling over the bay and stood mesmerized for a moment, admiring the hawk's ability to ride the thermal air currents like a surfer rides a wave. A movement in the yard shifted her attention away from the hawk. Out of the corner of her eye, about ten feet from the French doors, she saw a baby myna bird who'd fallen out of its nest. Every spring the myna birds built a nest in the giant bird of paradise in the garden outside Sam and Jessica's bedroom. Some mornings while having her coffee on the lanai, she watched them return to the nest with food for their babies over the past few weeks, but they were nowhere in sight the last couple of days. She wondered if they might have become victims of the hawk, since previously one of them was never far from the nest and mynas were very territorial. The only explanation that made sense to her was the hawk being responsible for their disappearance.

She knew if the hawk saw the baby myna in the grass, the chick would most likely suffer the same fate as its parents. So, she quickly went out one of the French doors into the garden and scooped him up and brought the chick back inside the house to safety. While Jessica's plate was full with Sam and Pua, she couldn't ignore the defenseless creature. A random act of kindness, while minimal to her, meant everything to the helpless chick that morning.

Jessica didn't know anything about raising birds and went online for information about how to care for a baby myna bird. She read the list of requirements: Put bird in a shoe box with a heating pad. Okay. Feed bird every thirty minutes. No, not happening. She glanced over at the baby bird, "It's not looking good for you, pal."

She grabbed a rice bag out of the freezer, and put it in the microwave oven for a minute. The warm bag in a shoe box would work as a temporary home for the little bird.

Earlier in the month, Jessica remembered reading an article in the newspaper about a local man who took care of injured birds, so she called the paper to get his name and contact information in hopes he might be willing to take over care of the chick.

Jessica made a phone call to the bird man and arranged for him to come pick up the baby myna.

Later that day, the man arrived in an old Dodge truck built in the early 1950s. The paint job was comprised of a hodge-podge of colorful birds painted all over it with the original rusty brown base color. He brought an adult myna bird with him and told the bird to shush when it started spewing four-letter words as he stepped out of the old truck. He was too far away for Jessica to hear what the bird said, but apparently the man didn't want to hear any more of it.

"I don't need a myna bird, I need you to take a myna bird," Jessica said.

"Bitch," the bird replied.

"Quiet, that's not nice," the bird man told the myna.

"No worries, lady, I'll take the chick." And the bird man took the shoe box and started walking back to his truck.

"Wait. On second thought, is your bird for sale?"

The bird man nodded.

"I'll take him." And Jessica wrote the man a check.

"What's his name?"

"Pilau. When I got him, he stunk to high heaven, so that's what I named him," the bird man said.

Though she didn't care much for the bird's vocabulary, he reminded her of a bird her dad used to have when she was growing up and thought maybe it would be a pleasant reminder of her father to have around. The name Pilau seemed to fit, but they would need to work on his calling her a bitch.

Jessica took Pilau inside and placed him on the parrot stand in the living room before she went to make the arrangements for Sam. But she did give him a word of advice before leaving. "Look out for the cat."

She didn't think Mr. Jangles would eat him, but Pilau didn't know that.

"What do you say now, smart-ass?" Jessica said.

"I love you baby," the myna shot back.

"That's better," she said, as she walked out the front door.

13

———————

S am opened his eyes and didn't know where he was or what happened to him. Jessica was asleep in a chair next to his bed. Her hand rested on top of his, her arm supported by the bed. The hospital wrist band, and the heart rate monitor on a stand next to him, cleared up any doubts in his mind as to where he was, after quickly surveying himself and the room.

For the past few months Sam had taken more and more pain pills trying to keep his excruciating back pain under control. The pills weren't working anymore, no matter how many he swallowed at a time. But one thing they could still do was kill him and they almost did.

Jessica felt Sam's hand move when he woke, and she gently squeezed it. She watched him look around and didn't say a word until he asked her, "What happened?"

Jessica's bloodshot eyes welled up with tears as she spoke, "Honey, if the gardener hadn't found you, you'd be dead now."

Sam's brow furrowed. It mystified him as to what happened.

"All I know is that I was sitting on the lanai watching the

canoe paddlers in the bay and my back was killing me, so I took a pain pill. How long have I been out?"

"Since yesterday," Jessica answered.

"I must have had some kind of reaction to the medication I've been taking."

Jessica ignored his last sentence and started to say something about kicking the addiction but stopped when the door opened. Dr. Chay entered the room and introduced himself to Sam, and Jessica excused herself and said she was going to the ladies' room. Earlier in the day, the doctor and Jessica agreed it was time for an intervention.

After the doctor checked Sam's vitals, he said, "Mr. Stewart, I would suggest you enter drug rehab after you leave the hospital."

Sam couldn't believe what he heard the doctor say. It was like a bad dream. Him a drug addict, who did this doctor think he was talking to?

Dr. Chay continued, "You're going to die. It's up to you whether it's going to be sooner or later. I've given your wife all the information on the facility to call. Do you have any questions before I release you?"

"Can you give me something for my back pain?"

Dr. Chay sighed, "Mr. Stewart, let me be clear. If you ever take another pain pill stronger than an aspirin, you're probably going to overdose. You should have died this time. Why you didn't is beyond me. I wish you well." He shook Sam's hand and left the room to continue on his rounds.

"Wow, what's up with him? I don't think I'm that bad," Sam mumbled to himself after Chay was gone.

Jessica waited down the hall until the doctor left Sam's room before she came back to the room.

All signs of the teary-eyed wife disappeared and were replaced by the serious, all business, she's-going-to-kick-his-ass wife when she returned to his bedside.

She said something he didn't expect, "I found all your

prescriptions–I'll cut to the chase. I called every one of your mainland doctors and told them if they so much as prescribe you anything more than an aspirin I'll see to it the DEA investigates them up close and personal, as if they were getting a rectal exam."

She smiled and lightly squeezed Sam's hand.

Sam's secret was out, and now he didn't have any choice other than to deal with it.

14

———

S ober five years, Jessica knew from experience everything coming out of Sam's mouth related to his drug use was likely pure bullshit and would be until he was clean for a while. If he stayed clean, that was.

The doctor released Sam later that morning and as they drove down the hill from the hospital toward Keauhou, Jessica said, "Don't worry, you're not going to rehab."

Sam sighed, "Well, that's the first good news I've heard today."

When she passed the turnoff to go home, he asked, "Where are we going."

"The airport, you're going to stay with Uncle Frank for a while. I can't go with you; I have to stay here and find out who killed Charles. Pua needs me, her I can help–you, I can't. Mike's waiting for you at the plane, it's fueled and ready to leave."

Sam peered out the window while looking at the ocean, but quickly turned his head back toward Jessica and said,

"What if I refuse to go?"

"If you don't go, I'll take Henry and leave you because you will die if you don't stop taking pain pills. I'm not going to be around to watch when it happens. It's that simple."

Sam sighed and thought for a moment, "I'm not an addict, but I'll do this for you and Henry."

"Uncle Frank will be waiting for you when you land in Bullhead and you'll be staying with him until he sees fit to send you back to me."

After a few minutes of silence Jessica continued,

"I told Mike if you order him to divert from Bullhead City to anywhere else to let me know. In case you're thinking of telling Mike otherwise, I'm expecting a call from Uncle Frank in about six hours saying he has picked you up. If I don't get the call, I won't be here when you return."

Jessica's only choice was to play hardball with Sam. The only way to motivate him to try hard enough to kick the addiction would be to make clear the consequences if he didn't. The survival of their relationship would be up to him going forward.

Captain Mike Johnson finished the pre-flight on the Gulfstream jet and was ready to go when Jessica dropped Sam off at the bottom of the plane's staircase. The flight attendant stood by on the ramp next to the stairs ready to help Sam board if he needed help, but he waved her off.

Sam loved Jessica and Henry more than anything else in the world, and the thought of her taking Henry and leaving him caused an agonizing pain, in the pit of his stomach, every time his mind thought about losing them. While he believed she and Dr. Chay were overreacting, he also thought going to Uncle Frank's for a while was a minor price to pay to keep the peace at home and get the heat off.

Three hours into the flight, an odd thing happened at forty thousand feet over the Pacific. Sam realized the sciatic pain in the muscles down his leg disappeared, now replaced by a weird flutter every once in a while. Maybe the nerve burned out, but whatever caused the pain to disappear was fine with him. Finally, relief from the pain for the first time in a long while.

A couple of hours later, he looked out the window while the jet descended as it crossed over the Colorado River and turned toward final approach into Bullhead City located on the Arizona side of the river. Laughlin was on the Nevada side, where he saw a row of hotel and gambling casinos along the riverbank.

Uncle Frank had been sober a long time, but Sam could never understand why he lived out in the middle of the desert. In the summer it was so hot the devil went back to hell because it was cooler there. And in the winter the wind blew constantly, so much so, the place should have been called the real windy city.

Uncle Frank stood outside the terminal smoking a cigarette when the Gulfstream jet rolled to a stop on the tarmac. Sam looked through the window and could see his uncle standing there. The old man looked like a dragon as he exhaled the smoke out his nostrils.

It was obvious to him his uncle had made a deal with the devil. He was in his seventies and still smoked like a chimney and didn't look like he was planning on slowing down or dying anytime soon.

Sam had concluded his body must have been too toxic an environment for cancer to survive in and marveled at his uncle's ability to beat the odds of dying from it.

Uncle Frank was more likely to die of a jealous husband, from what Sam recalled his mother saying to his father when he was a young boy. His mother had called his uncle "Filthy

Frank" more than once to his face, and he seemed to wear it as a badge of honor.

After the plane parked, and the wheels were chocked, the flight attendant opened the door for Sam and quickly moved away from the opening as a blast of scorching air came rushing into the cabin of the plane. When Sam stepped onto the tarmac of the Bullhead City Airport, he was certain he had arrived in Hell. It was so hot he could hardly breathe.

The sooner Sam could convince his uncle there was nothing to be worried about, the sooner he could get out of that hellhole and return home. But first he needed a good night of sleep.

15

———

The annual dinner cruise and fundraiser for the Kona animal shelter sold out early just like it always had. Every year the Murphy ohana attended the gala affair to contribute to the cause.

The event was being held that evening on the hundred and fifty passenger dinner boat, named the *Star of Kona*, that sailed nightly from the Kailua pier.

The locals referred to it as the booze cruise. On nights when the wind shifted, residents could hear the bongo drums a half-mile inland as the boat shadowed the Kona coast and the party raged onboard.

After Jessica got sober, she didn't make it a habit of going to slippery places with alcohol, and the booze cruise was about as slippery as it got for her. She reminded herself that was then, and this was now, and it was for a good cause. And no matter what, there wouldn't be any drinking of alcohol on her part. The uneasiness was well-founded and based on a previous incident.

Six years before on a visit home to see the family, before she quit drinking, she had taken part in debauchery of the highest level with a bongo drummer while in the women's bathroom onboard the *Star of Kona.*

That was the last time she had been on the boat. As she waited in a long line to board with Pua and Uncle Jack, she nervously bit her bottom lip as she scanned the boat's crew who were gathered next to the gangway assisting passengers.

She didn't see the bongo drummer, as she prayed he had moved on and wouldn't be there that evening. Before getting sober, there had been other moments of indiscretion after she drank too much. In LA, the chances of running into the same person again after such an escapade were minuscule. But Kona was a small town and it wasn't a matter of if but when, while the other party still lived on the island.

Larry and Erica Black were the last to arrive and almost missed the boat. Out of the fifteen tables in the dining room there were only two empty seats left and they were across from the Murphy table.

After being seated, Larry flashed a devilish grin at Jessica when their eyes met. He had dropped a few hints in the past that he would like their relationship to be more than just business, but she always ignored them. When Pua saw Erica sitting straight across from her she said to Jessica, "I'm going topside." She spent the rest of the evening above deck taking in the view so she wouldn't be sorry for anything she might say to Erica, since she had strict orders from her lawyer to stay out of trouble while out on bail.

Jessica had no interest in cheating on Sam, and if she had it wouldn't have been with Larry. She had told Sam to make sure all his deals with Larry were squeaky clean because it wouldn't be long before Larry was either in jail or dead due to his ties with the Russian mob. And when that day came, the Feds would be investigating all of Larry's business partners which guaranteed they'd be looking hard at Sam.

Jessica didn't love Sam because he was rich, she loved him because he had a good heart and he made her laugh. It was nice that he was wealthy, but if he lost his fortune it wouldn't be a deal breaker for her. Unlike Larry's wife, Erica, who only stayed with him for the money, property and prestige.

❦

It was dusk and the sky was bright from a near full moon as the *Star of Kona* departed from the pier. It cruised south along the coastline at a leisurely eight knots while being escorted by a pair of dolphins jumping and frolicking in front of the boat as it made its way down the coast. Seas were calm, and palm trees along the shoreline gently swayed in the balmy breeze as if doing the hula. The lights from homes dotted Mount Hualalai while they overlooked the coast and twinkled in the distance.

Besides the fundraiser there was an awards ceremony scheduled that evening. Larry and Erica Black were to be recognized for their donation of land where the new animal shelter was to be built.

The donation didn't come from the goodness of Larry's heart; the real reason behind his charity was the ancient Hawaiian burials discovered by the land surveyors after he had purchased the property. The burials prevented him from building the three hundred condos he had initially planned to place there.

The land was no longer feasible for commercial development but would make a great animal shelter and dog park, which Kona desperately needed. It wasn't all downside for Larry's real estate company as the donation would give him a lot of free publicity and a huge tax deduction.

After the *Star of Kona* got underway it didn't take long for Larry to come to the Murphy table and ask Jessica where Sam was. She offered a quick, "He went to the mainland on business," and nothing more. Larry took the hint and moved on to the next table to mingle.

When Jessica turned back from Larry, she noticed Uncle Jack staring at Erica. "You know her?" she asked.

"Yes, I had a buddy that dated her years ago, he said she's dangerous. He met her in a club we used to drink at. If I remember right, she worked in a couple of different clubs I used to frequent in Honolulu back then."

"Dangerous, how so?"

"He said she almost killed him one night when they got into a fight. According to him she had a mean left hook that wasn't giving her the desired result, so she grabbed a lamp off the table in his apartment and almost cracked his skull with it. He said it took fifty stitches to close the gash on the side of his head."

Jessica nodded, leaned forward and took a sip of her iced tea, then slid back into the chair.

"I see the gears working," Uncle Jack said, as he looked at Jessica.

She shook her head while stirring her salad with a fork, "It's probably nothing. I just have a lot on my plate right now with Sam and everything."

"I heard you packed him off to Laughlin?"

Jessica nodded as she took another sip of tea.

"Yes, he's with his Uncle Frank. He'll be back in a couple of weeks–did your friend file a police report?"

"I don't know, I'll find out."

16

U ncle Frank's suite at the Riverside Resort overlooked the RV park on the mountain side of the road. The Colorado River flowed by the hotel on the other side of the building, which sat at the water's edge.

Sam never understood why Uncle Frank lived in a suite at the hotel instead of a regular house; Lord knows he had enough money. But the old guy just liked that hotel for some reason, and had been living there for the past six months, after selling his casino and moving down from Vegas.

Sam sat up in bed, while looking out the window from the sixteenth floor of the hotel. Every cell in his body was screaming for relief from the Vicodin withdrawal he was going through. Every muscle in his body hurt. He felt so bad, in fact, that he thought it wouldn't be far from the truth to say even his hair hurt. It had been seventy-two hours since he had overdosed and almost killed himself accidentally. And now he was thinking he just needed a little 'hair of the dog' to get right with the world. Just one pill, to take the edge off, was all he needed and maybe then he would think about getting off the pills.

Since Jessica had packed Sam's suitcase, he was sure she

would have looked for his emergency stash and flushed it when she found it. After rolling out of bed and checking his bag just in case she missed it, Sam started to head for the shower, when Uncle Frank entered the room holding two large, steaming cups of coffee.

Just in case Sam had the shakes, Frank handed him a cup only half filled. Then his uncle sat in the chair at the desk, across from the bed, and turned it to face Sam. The old guy lit a cigarette, deeply inhaled, and blew smoke out of his nostrils like a dragon, while he stared at Sam for a moment before he took a sip of coffee.

The smell of cigarette smoke made Sam even more nauseous. Uncle Frank had been sober a long time, and smoked more often than not, and Sam knew asking him to put out his cigarette was a non-starter. Sam didn't say anything, and would let his uncle do all the talking, while he thought about ways to come up with some Vicodin.

After a minute of staring at each other, while they sipped their coffee, Uncle Frank broke the ice.

"Morning Sam, I suspect right about now your body is craving something to make it feel better–Vicodin most likely." Sam nodded and continued to just listen for the time being.

"I will take you to meetings with me for the next thirty days. And then we'll see where you are at that point." Frank sat his coffee cup down on the desk behind him and pulled an AA meeting schedule out of his back pocket. He looked at it for a couple of minutes, while his cigarette hung out of the corner of his mouth, and the smoke swirled toward the ceiling.

Uncle Frank stood up and turned his back toward Sam so he could get more light from the window to read the meeting guide. Sam studied the black Tommy Bahama shirt the old man was wearing and admired the palm tree design embroidered into the fabric on the back. He thought it odd that a guy who lived in the desert always wore aloha shirts, and he, who actually lived in Hawaii, seldom did. Sam was a tank top, board shorts and rubber slipper kind of guy most of the time in Kona. He was proud to be one of Hawaii's most casual billionaires. He rarely, however, wore a tank top at home, and with his tanned skin and six-pack abs, he never got an argument from Jessica. As far as he knew, she didn't care if he ever wore a shirt again.

Frank put his cigarette out and stuffed the meeting schedule back in his pocket.

"This addiction you have kills rich people just as dead as it does poor people. So, if your plan is to think your way out of this, you're screwed," Frank said, as a matter of fact.

Sam frowned and continued to sip his coffee. He decided not to say a word, until Uncle Frank handed him a couple of aspirin, that he'd forgotten to give him earlier.

"Thanks," Sam said, as he reached for them.

Sam wasn't going to be able to buy his way out of this and, deep down inside, he had a feeling he was going to have to trust Uncle Frank. But for the time being, Sam just needed to get the heat off, and if going to AA meetings was going to get everyone off his back, he would do it. Or until he could get a new doctor to write a script.

17

───────

It was 4:30 a.m. and Pua awoke hot and sweaty. Not only was her life falling apart, her house too. The air conditioner had broken the week before and the repairman said it would be at least another week until he could get to it.

One of the benefits Pua enjoyed from waking up so early was the quiet. The only thing she heard was the surf rolling in and breaking against the shoreline a few hundred yards down the hill from her home.

The air inside the house was humid and too hot for Pua to go back to sleep. She got up and went out to the lanai to see if it was any cooler. She sighed with relief when a cool breeze, coming off the mountain, gently cooled her skin as she sat down in the recliner pointed toward the coast. Even if she couldn't sleep, it was okay if she just sat there and stared at the moonlight shining brightly on the ocean. The smell of salt in the air and the sound of the sea in the distance soothed her soul.

She sat in her easy chair, with her eyes closed, and pondered where she had gone wrong since Charles' murder. She'd regretted ignoring Amanda Lee months earlier when the reporter had asked her to call.

Maybe giving her an interview would have helped soften the tone of the article Lee wrote about Pua Murphy Property Management allowing the rental property fund to be stolen as a result of sloppy bookkeeping.

As she continued to stare at the ocean, she thought about the loss the day before in small claims court. The same judge found in favor of all the former clients that previously sued her for the money Charles embezzled.

At that point, Pua had appeared in court over twenty times and each time the judge ruled against her. At the rate the losses had mounted, the only way she could afford to pay the judgments would be to sell her home. By her estimation, there was just enough equity in it to reimburse everyone who sued her.

The issue wasn't that she didn't want to pay them, the problem was she didn't have the money. And she would still be on the hook for Lori Makani's fees if her case went to trial. All the big deals she had in the pipeline dried up after news of the embezzlement. Worst-case scenario, she could liquidate her share in Aloha Village if necessary, but hoped it wouldn't come to that.

Later that morning she opened her email to find an estimate from the air conditioning company for nine thousand dollars to replace the air conditioning in her building. She thought about how she was going to come up with it when the phone rang; it was Lori Makani.

"I have some news Pua, I just came from a meeting with the DA, Ms. King. She's offering you a plea bargain of twenty years for manslaughter in exchange for a guilty plea. Otherwise, you're looking at life in prison if you get convicted of murdering Charles."

There was a brief silence on the line as Pua thought about what to say.

"Tell her no thanks."

"Are you sure about that? You could be out in ten years with good behavior."

"I'm not voluntarily going to prison for a crime I didn't commit."

"I'm required by law to tell you what the DA offered. I agree, you shouldn't take the deal. King doesn't have a slam dunk case. While I think I can convince the jury there is reasonable doubt, you never know for sure what they're going to do. And the chances of one of them having a friend or relative that was a victim of Charles' fraud is pretty high since the jury pool is so small. That's the thing that scares me about going to trial."

After she hung up, Pua thought about what Lori said. A trial was the last thing she wanted to do, but it was inevitable. It was time to sell her stake in Aloha Village Resort and put her building on the market.

As Pua thought about losing everything, she almost wished the North Korea nuclear missile alert had been the real thing.

Two days later Pua sold her Mercedes to raise the cash needed to fix the broken air conditioner in her building. She had enough money left over from the sale of the car to buy a used Toyota Corolla.

A month later she sold her home-office building to a nice European couple who paid cash. In two months' time Pua managed to raise enough cash by liquidating her assets to pay all the judgments against her. Afterward, she used the money that remained to move into an apartment on Hamburger Hill, which locals had nicknamed as such because it was located up the road above a McDonalds.

Pua got a lesson in humility that she hadn't asked for and definitely hadn't wanted. But as she and Kainoa sat on the floor next to boxes, she listened to the rats run around in the ceiling and thought about the times she had been in worse situations. If she could stay out of prison–she could rebuild.

Kainoa spent most days with Uncle Jack, and though Pua hadn't asked him, she was sure he or Jessica would take Kainoa if she went to prison.

The only thing she had managed to salvage was her real estate license and the satisfaction that she had paid everyone back that Charles had ripped off. But she still had one last debt to pay.

18

———

Pua and her lawyer Lori Makani met at Jessica's house to settle up and talk about her upcoming trial. They sat at the table on the lanai overlooking Keauhou Bay and sipped iced tea while making small talk about the boats passing by, before they got down to business.

"I have the rest of your fee," Pua said, as she pulled it out of her purse and slid the hundred thousand dollar check across the table to Lori. Sam and Jessica had bought her stake in Aloha Village and promised they would let her buy it back someday if and when she could.

Jessica waited for Pua and Lori to conduct their business and after they were done, she said, "Unfortunately I haven't been able to come up with anything concrete that ties Erica to the murder. But Gabbie is looking into an assault charge filed against her in Honolulu." The look on Pua's face was grim; she had hoped Jessica had something more than a hunch that would prove her innocence.

Lori nodded, "Keep looking. I'm going to subpoena Erica and see if I can get the jury to believe she might have done it. We only need them to think she *might* have done it." Lori looked at Pua and said, "Remember they have to find you guilty beyond a reasonable doubt. I plan on showing them a truckload of doubt. But it's going to be tricky since we're not filing an alternate perpetrator defense."

W ith three months to go before the Hawaii County election for a new District Attorney, DA King was running for office against her boss and wanted every murder conviction she could get before the voting booths opened on election day. This time Pua Murphy wouldn't have her grandfather to pull strings to save her from justice.

On the first morning of the trial, Pua and Lori Makani sat at the defense table in the old Kona courthouse and listened to the DA's opening statement. The jury watched intently, except for the one old guy on the end of the jury box who at best appeared to be taking a nap, and at worst, had died and nobody had noticed yet.

Pua watched him to see if he moved, and after five minutes there was not so much as a wiggle. Seated next to him was an older woman who just glared at Pua the entire time Carrie King made her opening statement.

The DA had a good motive and witnesses who would swear they heard Pua threaten to kill Charles. Pua was in deep trouble, and she knew it–everyone knew it. Jessica sat in the front row of the gallery right behind her sister and listened to King's argument. By the time the prosecutor finished running Pua into the ground, it sounded like people would start referring to the victim, Charles Lim, as Saint Charles by the end of the trial. Never mind the fact he ripped off a lot of them for a hundred and fifty thousand dollars. But–he wasn't the one on trial.

Lori Makani, known as a great deal maker, avoided going to trial whenever possible. Ninety-nine percent of her clients were guilty and always took the plea agreement she worked

BONUS

Get the free prequel and new release notifications.
https://readerlinks.com/l/965413

out for them with the DA. Before the trial Pua was adamant she would not agree to make any deals, but was seriously starting to reconsider after the first morning in court.

As Pua's lawyer made her opening statement she stood near the jury box looking at each juror while she talked. When she got to the old guy at the end with his eyes closed, she stepped in front of him and dropped a five-hundred-page hardcover book she had been holding. The loud thud of it hitting the floor made his eyes pop wide open. He straightened up in his chair as Lori's eyes bore into his. Judge Sato looked up from taking notes and gave Ms. Makani a stern look but said nothing.

"My apologies, your Honor,"

She continued, "Yes, there were people who heard Pua Murphy threaten Charles Lim, but there isn't one shred of physical evidence tying her to the crime, and not one witness who saw her murder him. And that's because she didn't kill him. Yes, she had motive, but so did the forty-seven people who Charles stole deposits from."

As Ms. Makani continued her opening statement, Jessica felt her phone vibrate in her pocket. After glancing at the screen to see who it was, she went outside the courtroom to take the call. On the way out of the courtroom she noticed Larry Black sitting in the back of the room near the door. Their eyes met for just a moment as she passed by him. When she returned, Larry glanced over his shoulder as he heard the loud ca-chunk of the courtroom door latch open. He held out his hand with a note for Jessica as she walked past him.

"Call me" was scribbled on the small piece of paper and Jessica tucked it into her pocket as she walked back to her seat behind Pua. She sat there and wondered what Larry Black wanted to talk about as the judge reminded the jurors not to discuss the case and that court was in recess until the following day. Jessica heard the courtroom door latch snap shut and looked back over her shoulder and saw Larry's seat was empty, and he had left the room.

The next day of the trial Pua and Lori Makani sat at the defense table taking notes while DA Carrie King questioned Detective Kaipo.

"Detective, I have two more questions. When you arrived at the crime scene what did you find?"

"Charles Lim lying in a pool of blood; he'd been hit in the head with a shark's tooth club."

King nodded and followed up with, "What did Sue Carter and Lillian Pelekane tell you when you first arrived at the crime scene?"

"They said the day before the murder they heard Pua Murphy threaten to kill Charles Lim."

"I have just one last question detective. Did they tell you they saw any other witnesses?"

Kaipo nodded, "They said Jessica Kealoha was there at the bottom of the stairs."

"Thank you, detective. No further questions your Honor."

Judge Sato said, "Defense counsel, would you like to cross-examine this witness?"

Lori Makani stood, "Yes, your Honor."

"Detective Kaipo, you said earlier that there was a shark's tooth club lying next to the victim."

"Yes, that's true," Kaipo acknowledged.

"Was it the left side or the right side of the skull where the victim had been hit?"

"Looking at the victim it was the left side."

"Thank you, detective. No further questions," your Honor.

Just after court was adjourned for lunch, a young man

approached Jessica as she left the gallery with Pua and said, "Are you Jessica Kealoha?"

"Yes."

"You've been served," he said as he shoved a piece of paper toward her.

Jessica stopped and read it for a moment, and said to Pua as she put it in her purse, "I'm being called as a witness for the prosecution."

During the break Pua and Jessica went to Teshima's for lunch. The eatery was a couple of miles from the courthouse and the oldest Japanese restaurant in Kona.

Jessica pointed to the back corner of the dining hall when the hostess approached, "Can we please have that table?"

The hostess nodded and showed them to the small table. Jessica sat with her back against the wall like she always did and Pua turned her chair slightly toward the window, so she didn't have to stare at the wall.

When the waitress came to the table, they both ordered saimin and sat quietly waiting for their soup to arrive until Jessica broke the silence, "When the DA calls me to testify, I can't lie on the stand. I want to, but I can't."

Pua nodded, "I understand. I wouldn't want you to. I'm the one who threatened Charles publicly. Of course, I didn't mean it, but that doesn't matter now. It's what it sounds like that matters,"

The waitress brought a tray with their bowls of saimin and sat them down quickly and disappeared to deliver food to the other tables in the dining room. Jessica dipped her spoon in the bowl and blew on the steaming hot liquid and noodles. The saimin was too hot to eat, so she put the spoon back in the bowl, reached into her shirt pocket and pulled out a piece of paper which she laid on the table.

Pua slowly slurped her soup and watched as Jessica dialed the number written on the paper.

"What's up Larry?"

Jessica didn't say much other than "uh huh" for the minute and a half she was on the phone.

She hung up and said, "I don't want to get your hopes up, but there might be some new evidence that could exonerate you. Don't get excited yet, I'm going to meet Larry Black tomorrow to see it for myself first and then if it's true, we'll go from there."

"Jessica Kealoha!"

In response to the bailiff's booming voice, she got up from her seat in the gallery, right behind Pua, and walked to the front of the witness stand. After taking the oath she replied, "So help me God."

Jessica was the first witness called by DA King that morning. She had been on the stand hundreds of times over the years in her former career as a detective and never had butterflies when going to testify—but this time was different. Her words could help put her sister in prison for the rest of her life and her gut was nothing *but* butterflies mixed with guilt that morning.

Ms. King started her first question with, "Ms. Kealoha—"

Jessica interrupted, "Actually, it's Mrs. Stewart now."

The DA had a confused look on her face but continued, "My apologies—Mrs. Stewart, is it true, that the day before Charles Lim was murdered you witnessed your sister Pua Murphy threaten to kill him?"

Jessica stalled as long as she could before Judge Sato said, "Please answer the question."

Jessica turned her head toward the judge, nodded and reluctantly looked back at King, "Yes, but she didn't mean it."

"How do you know she didn't?"

"I think she was angry and used a poor choice of words to convey it, but I don't believe for a second she meant it?"

As King looked at the jury she said, "But the fact is she said it and Charles Lim was dead the next morning. No further questions your Honor."

Lori Makani stood up and approached Jessica, "Why is it you don't think Pua was serious about killing Charles?"

Jessica looked at the jury. "If she meant it, she wouldn't have said a word. Instead, she would have kicked him down the stairs right then. With a brown belt in karate, she wouldn't have had a problem doing that."

19

———————

It was the third day of the trial and the prosecution had called all of its witnesses and now it was Lori Makani's turn.

The bailiff called out, "Erica Black!"

In response, a tall, well-dressed woman seated in the back of the courtroom got up and strutted to the witness stand and was sworn in.

Lori Makani didn't waste any time going after her.

"Did you sign a prenup with Larry Black that said you'd get nothing if he found out you cheated on him?"

"Yes."

"Did you have an affair with Charles Lim?"

Erica glared at Ms. Makani and remained silent.

After a minute of silence, Ms. Makani looked to Judge Sato, who was busy typing on his computer, "Your Honor, please compel the witness to answer the question."

Judge Sato nodded, stopped typing and turned his attention toward the witness stand and said, "Mrs. Black, please answer the question."

Her brow narrowed, and she answered, "No, I did not."

The loud ca-chunk of the heavy courtroom doors interrupted the tension of the moment and Gabbie Harris walked down the aisle to the railing separating the gallery from the defense table. She waited for Ms. Makani to come to her.

"One moment your Honor, please."

Judge Sato nodded.

Gabbie handed a piece of paper to Ms. Makani and took a seat. The attorney smiled and walked back to where she was originally standing as she questioned Erica.

"Mrs. Black, have you ever been arrested for battery?"

The DA stood up and said, "Objection, your Honor, I don't see the relevance."

Lori Makani fired back, "Your Honor, I can show relevance in a moment."

Judge Sato said, "I'll allow it, but get to the point sooner rather than later."

Ms. Makani nodded and walked back toward Erica as she said, "Mrs. Black, I have a Honolulu Police report here that says ten years ago you were arrested for assault and battery. It says you attacked the victim and bashed him in the head with a lamp."

"Objection your Honor, I still fail to see the relevance," King protested.

"My point, your Honor, is Mrs. Black has a history of violence and could have killed Charles Lim. In the police report it says she hit the victim in the head with a lamp."

Loud whispers filled the courtroom so much so that Judge Sato banged his gavel until there was silence in the room.

Judge Sato called recess for lunch, but not before calling Lori Makani up to the bench and giving her a stern warning that she was walking a very fine line and best back up any further insinuations of Erica Black being involved in the murder with proof.

Lori and Pua had a meeting, outside the courthouse under a tree, to talk about how the trial was going, while Jessica left to meet with Larry Black at a bar called the Corner Pocket in Kealakekua.

"Even though the prosecution certainly hasn't proven beyond a shadow of a doubt you're guilty, we're losing," Lori said. Pua nodded and wrung her hands as she listened.

Lori continued, "I've been watching the jury, and they're not buying what we're selling."

Pua nodded and said, "Ask King if the deal's still on the table. I'd rather eventually get out than never."

"Are you sure? Maybe we should wait to see what Jessica thinks."

"Jessica's not the one going to have to do the time."

"Okay, I'll go see if I can track her down."

Lori left and Pua sat under the tree, as she tried not to cry, while she waited for Jessica to return.

Larry Black arrived early at the bar and sat at a table near the window while he waited for Jessica. Ten minutes later, when she walked in the door, he stood and waved until her eyes adjusted to the darkness and she recognized him. When she sat at the table, the smell of vodka from Larry's drink jolted her for a moment. After five years of not drinking, the odor of alcohol was repugnant to her, but she did her best to ignore it so she could get down to business.

Larry waved at the waitress, but Jessica shook her head, waved her off and said, "I don't have long, why am I here?"

"Okay, suit yourself. I have something I think will help your sister's case," Larry said as he pulled a small voice recorder out of his shirt pocket and laid it on the table next to his drink.

"I have a recording of Erica yelling at Charles just before she killed him. There's a time stamp on the audio, it's the morning of the murder. You can hear her say 'you son-of-a-bitch.' Then you hear him say 'put that down,' which I assume meant that she had grabbed the club off the wall that he was killed with. The next thing you hear is what sounds like her hitting him twice with it and then there's no more sound other than the bells on the office door when she opened it to leave."

Jessica looked up and caught the waitress' attention as she was passing by and asked, "Can I get a glass of water please?"

"Of course, I'll be right back."

Jessica turned back to Larry and said, "What's in this for you?"

"Erica goes to prison for life and I get a divorce where I don't have to pay her one red cent. That's what's in it for me."

"How did you bug her?"

"For her birthday I gave her a new Louis Vuitton purse that had a recorder embedded in it." Larry smiled, while pausing for a moment to take a sip of his drink, then continued, "The plan was to remove the miniature recorder once a week when she was sleeping and download the audio. I got it after you and Gabbie couldn't get a photo of her and Charles together. It's yours, take it." Larry slid the recorder across the table to Jessica.

She stared at the recorder as she tapped her index finger on the table for a minute before she asked, "Why now and not months ago?"

"The purse was stolen a couple of weeks after I gave it to her and was recovered recently. Three days ago was the first time I was able to download the recording of her and Charles. There were other recordings of her and some other guy having sex. That's the proof I needed, so I'm giving you what you need to solve your problem and mine."

When they returned from lunch, Pua, Jessica, and Lori met outside the courthouse before going back inside.

"Well?" Pua asked as Lori approached her.

"No deal."

"You better not be making any deals," Jessica demanded as she joined the other two. She smiled and pulled the voice recorder out of her pocket and said, "Listen to this."

That afternoon, after the recording was entered into evidence, DA Carrie King dropped the murder charge against Pua, and Judge Sato dismissed the case.

After the case was dismissed and the sisters had a long emotional hug, they invited Lori to the Kona Inn to celebrate with drinks and mud pie. It was a perfect late afternoon on the outside lanai of the world-famous restaurant overlooking Kailua Bay. The place was busy that day, as there was a cruise ship in port, and Kailua Village was running over with tourists.

The trio sat at a table in the corner, closest to the water, just like they had many times before in the early years of their lives growing up in Kona.

The soft sounds of slack key guitar filled the air over the outdoor patio–it was a juxtaposition of the sterile courtroom they had just come from.

"That was a close call," Pua said, as she lifted her glass to make a toast. Jessica and Lori joined her, "To freedom," and they clinked their glasses together.

They sat and told stories about growing up in Kona, and the fun times they had, until after sunset. As the manager lit the tiki torches, Jessica proclaimed it was time for her to go. "Okay, I'm the designated driver." Pua and Lori nodded, agreed a good time was had by all and that it was time to go.

20

Pua was broke, her reputation in shambles and her business was all but destroyed. Through it all she managed to keep her real estate license and still had a way to make a living, if she could get more new clients. Since the trial, her phone hadn't rung much, and it didn't ring at all when she was under indictment.

One morning a few days after the trial she was at Starbucks out by the harbor, having a pumpkin spice latte and checking out what was going to be her new office, when her phone rang. She hoped it wasn't a telemarketer like the two previous calls. At first glance it didn't look good; she didn't recognize the caller's name or number, and it had a mainland area code which meant half the time it was someone trying to sell her something.

"Aloha, this is Pua Murphy."

"Hi, I'm Ian Petrovsky," the caller said with a Russian accent. "I'm calling about a property you have listed for sale on Kaloko Drive."

"Great," Pua thought to herself. This particular property had been on the market for a couple of years and belonged to a crusty old mechanic named Bob Jensen, who hated real

estate agents with a passion. It was the only listing she had left and though she wasn't crazy about the client, she needed to make some money.

Petrovsky was responding to an ad Pua had placed on Craigslist the day before. *"Thank God,"* she thought to herself, when Petrovsky told her he was calling about the house for sale.

The property was well taken care of and Bob Jensen wouldn't settle for anything less than top dollar. As a result, it sat on the market and no amount of persuasion about the price being too high would change Bob's mind, because he didn't care what Pua or anybody else thought. He wanted what he wanted and that was all there was to it.

Since he had turned down more than one decent offer over the last year, Pua had hoped he'd just take the place off the market and quit wasting her time, but now she was grateful to have the listing. She agreed to show the house to Mr. Petrovsky as soon as she could arrange it with "Old Grumpy," as she liked to refer to him.

Petrovsky was only going to be on the island for another couple of days and wanted to see it as soon as possible.

Pua dialed Bob and as she listened to the phone ring she thought *"I hope he'll let me show it today."*

She expected a less than cooperative attitude, but it surprised her that, for the first time, he sounded somewhat reasonable and didn't require the usual twenty-four hours' notice.

"Sure, bring your looky-loo on over. And make sure he has more than two nickels to rub together. Lucky for you, I just cleaned the damn place, otherwise I would've told you to forget it."

Normally, Pua always prequalified anyone she took to "Old Grumpy's" house because he insisted on it. But there wasn't time, she needed to make a sale, so she rolled the dice and hoped Bob wouldn't ask about it like he usually did when they arrived to look at the property.

I an Petrovsky arrived at the harbor Starbucks an hour later and met with Pua. They took his rental car to see the property since she didn't think her old Toyota could climb the 7.6 percent incline up Kaloko Drive.

Pua made it a rule to never ride alone with new male clients, but that year was full of things she had never done, so to increase her safety she said to Petrovsky when he arrived, "A couple of things: the house we're going to see is at the top of a very steep road and I don't think my car will make it. And two, I'm going to take a photo of you and send it to my sister, so she knows whom to find if I disappear. Okay?"

He nodded and said, "Make sure you get my good side," then smiled while she took the photo.

When they arrived, Bob Jensen was sticking pink flamingos in the ground around the front yard. Pua swore anything to make the neighbors mad was his motto. And he was good at it. Pua heard more than once they all wished he'd sell and go make someone else's life miserable for a change.

Bob Jensen was the only client Pua ever had that wouldn't go somewhere and wait while the property was being shown, not Old Grumpy. He wanted to eyeball every potential buyer that came to look at his place. The only reason she put up with his nonsense was because he was the best mechanic on the island, and he had saved her from being stranded in Waipio Valley when her vehicle wouldn't start. It was late afternoon and darkness was approaching. A couple of backyard mechanics had already tried and failed to get her 4Runner to start, but Bob had it running in five minutes, just as the sun set. He said it was a temporary fix and it would get her home, but to bring it to his shop in the morning, and he would perform a proper long-term repair. If Pua had known what a pain-in-the-ass client he would turn out to be, she might have decided to take her chances in Waipio Valley when the 4Runner wouldn't start.

W hen Pua and Ian Petrovsky pulled in the driveway, and she saw the pink flamingos, she started to cry. It was just too much. What had she done to deserve this? She was sure God had it in for her. That's all she could figure, and Bob Jensen had been put on Earth to torture her. Petrovsky stopped the car in the driveway and said, "What's the matter?" Pua pointed at the plastic flamingos.

She had held up well while being tried for murder, going to small claims court on a weekly basis and selling everything she owned to pay her debts. But the pink flamingos put her over the edge. She had made up her mind, she was going to fire Bob Jensen as a client. Then Mr. Petrovsky said something she never expected, "I love those things," as he pointed at the cheap plastic birds.

Pua grabbed a napkin out of her purse and dabbed her eyes as she said, "I do too."

Ian Petrovsky was a Russian immigrant who had been in the US five years. It just so happened pink flamingos were his favorite bird, and he had Pua write a full price offer that day for Bob Jensen's property.

21

———————

S am had gone to AA meetings in Bullhead City with Uncle Frank for thirty days and gotten his 30-day chip–and it was time to go home.

"Okay kid, you're as ready as you're ever going to be," Uncle Frank said, as he drove Sam to the airport.

Uncle Frank's parting words were, "Remember, don't take any more of those pills, even if your ass falls off."

Sam smiled and nodded as he walked to the plane, thinking he was too smart to ever let another pain pill get the better of him. A few minutes later the jet climbed out of Bullhead City and made a right turn over the Colorado River toward Hawaii.

J essica and Henry sat in the 4Runner on the ramp at the Kona airport, and watched planes take off and land while they waited for Sam's plane. During the time leading up to Pua's trial, Jessica wasn't able to spend much time with Henry, and she'd been trying to make up for it the past few weeks by taking him everywhere with her.

It was nice having Auntie May at the house whenever she needed her, but Jessica didn't want to become one of those mothers that let the nanny raise her child.

"Look," Jessica pointed at the Gulfstream jet that just landed and was taxiing toward the ramp.

"I see it, I see it," Henry said excitedly as he pointed at the plane as it approached. There was no mistaking the plane with the name Jessica, in gold leaf, on the side of the fuselage.

Henry reached for the door handle, but Jessica grabbed him, "Let's wait until the plane comes to a stop, okay?"

As the jet rolled to a stop Jessica said, "Okay, we can get out now, but sit tight and I'll come around and get you." Henry did as he was told and waited for Jessica to open the door.

Jessica had Henry by the hand while they anxiously waited for the door of the plane to open.

"Let's stay right here," Jessica said, as she held Henry's hand firmly. She felt him tug, as the anticipation made him want to run to the plane.

The ground crew, from Air Services, chocked the wheels as the fuel truck pulled around to the other side of the plane.

"Come on Henry," Jessica said, as she held his hand and they walked toward the plane.

Sam bolted from the doorway and rushed down the stairs to pick up Henry. Balanced on Sam's arm, Henry wrapped his arms around Sam's neck, as Sam leaned over to kiss Jessica.

"I missed you guys so much," Sam said, his smile big and genuine as they walked to the 4Runner.

"You look good," Jessica said, as she stared into Sam's eyes and returned the smile.

"I feel good. Let's go home, I can't wait to meet... what's the bird's name?" "Pilau," Jessica said, as she laughed.

Sam carried Henry to the passenger side of the truck, hopped in the back seat with him, and kept his arm around his shoulder during the drive home.

When Jessica pulled in the driveway, she said, "My dad had a talking myna bird, and it just seemed like a good idea at the time when I got Pilau. He has quite a vocabulary. Luckily, he only knows a couple of bad words and I've told Henry they are not to be repeated."

Henry nodded and said, "I'm not allowed to say the "B" word that Pilau says."

Sam did his best to keep from laughing. "Let's go see him."

Pilau was on his perch in the living room when Sam walked in the door. "Say hello to Sam," Jessica told the bird as she walked by him headed to the kitchen. "Sam's the man, Sam's the man," Pilau said. Sam smiled, "I like that bird; he's pretty smart. Now I have to go sit on the lanai and stare at the bay for a while, soak in the view and let my skin soak up the humidity. Right now it feels like a prune after spending a month in the desert."

Sam walked to the chair closest to the ocean and sighed as he sat down. It felt as if he'd been gone a million years.

The next morning, he sat in his favorite chair on the lanai, overlooking Keauhou Bay, while he read the Wall Street Journal. Jessica was inside the house getting ready to meet Pua for coffee at Lava Java. After she checked herself in the mirror and put on a new lip balm she had never tried before, she walked outside to the lanai and kissed Sam on the lips. He noticed something immediately different, the taste of her caramel-flavored lip balm. Two things Sam loved most... Jessica and caramel.

He sat the paper down, stood up from his chair and spread his well-toned arms to invite Jessica in for a hug. He had a devilish grin and scanned the yard to make sure Henry hadn't come out of the house, and said, "Why don't you coat yourself with that, and I'll lick it off later, when Auntie May takes Henry to Aloha Village for the day?"

Jessica put her forehead to his and murmured, "I'll use real caramel later. But right now, I'm off to meet Pua for coffee at Lava Java. What are your plans this morning honey?"

"The rusty weathervane on top of the house needs to be removed. Today it gets dealt with. I called a handyman a few minutes ago; he's supposed to come over later this morning to take it down. The people that originally built this house owned a poultry conglomerate on the mainland, so I guess that's why they had a chicken as a weathervane."

"Too bad, I kind of liked that rusty chicken up there," Jessica replied.

"How about a sailboat instead?" Sam asked.

"No sailboats," Jessica snapped.

Sam raised an eyebrow, "Okay, no sailboats."

Jessica caught herself. "I'm sorry honey, not sure where that came from."

"How about a dolphin or marlin instead?" Sam asked.

"I love dolphins," Jessica said, as she picked up her purse to leave.

"Dolphins it is," Sam said, and went back to reading the paper.

"Anything interesting in the paper?"

"There is an IPO for a new tech company that I'm interested in. They've developed a buoy that generates electricity while floating on the surface of the ocean."

Sam's eyes lit up whenever he talked about new technology and the ocean.

"I'd love to hear the rest of it, honey, but I have to be at Lava Java in fifteen minutes, so I have to go."

Sam nodded and felt a sharp pain in his lower back as he shifted in the chair to kiss Jessica goodbye. It had been the first serious pain since he'd gotten clean, and he thought, *"I hope there isn't more to come."*

22

———————

P ua arrived first at Lava Java and had a table in the back tucked away, off to the side and back from the road, with a peek-a-boo view of Kailua Bay.

The restaurant was busy; there was canoe racing that weekend and teams from all over the island were in town to compete.

Pua stood and waved at Jessica when she saw her near the hostess station at the front of the restaurant. Jessica nodded and zig-zagged her way through the crowded tables to the back.

"Sorry I couldn't get a table up front," Pua said.

"No worries, I like this better. Less road noise and car exhaust to suck down with my coffee."

Jessica looked around for a moment after she sat down, "They've expanded; it's nice."

Pua nodded, "The last time I was here was when the false missile alert happened, and Charles told me he stole the money." Her face grew solemn. "Enough about that, how's Sam?" Pua asked, as she watched the waitress deliver a plate of banana pancakes to a nearby table. Her expression changed to one of happiness.

"He looks good. He's home with Henry waiting for the handyman to arrive. He's having the guy change the weather-vane on top of the house."

"Good, that thing was tacky," Pua laughed.

"I know, but I kind of overreacted when he asked me if I wanted to put up a sailboat to replace it."

Pua's face turned serious, "Maybe a little lingering PTSD?"

"Probably. I apologized and we agreed on a dolphin instead."

Pua's expression softened but she said nothing.

"Don't worry, I'm fine. It's probably about time for a tune-up with the shrink," Jessica laughed.

Pua smiled and nodded, then cut her eyes toward the front of the dining room and jutted her chin in that direction. Jessica turned to see what had grabbed Pua's attention. Usually, it was some amazing food being delivered, but this time it was Erica Black.

"More coffee?" the waitress asked, as she stopped at the table. Jessica pushed her cup over to get a refill and Pua said, "Yes, please, and banana pancakes."

"Sure, and how about you?" the woman said to Jessica.

Before she could answer Pua said, "Go ahead, I'm buying, I just sold a house."

Jessica smiled and said, "With coconut syrup."

"Comin' right up."

After the waitress left, Pua said, "Looks like Erica made bail. When's her trial supposed to start, do you know?"

Jessica shook her head, "I have no idea. But it won't be long until Kona is rid of the likes of her. I heard Larry's already filed for divorce."

Pua heaved out a sigh, "I'll try not to gloat. But really, I'm trying to be a better person these days. Nothing like losing all my stuff and almost my freedom to impart a serious change of attitude about what's important in life."

Jessica smiled and nodded; she liked the changes she saw in Pua–all for the better.

"After we eat, let's walk down toward the pier, We can watch the canoes finish, and I want to see how Freddie's doing," Jessica said.

❀

It had been years since the last time Pua and Jessica had strolled through the village and Jessica noted, as they walked by the jewelry shop across from the breakwater, "The Moreton Bay fig tree looks the same as it did when we were kids."

"Moreton Bay? I always thought it was a magnolia tree," Pua laughed. Jessica smirked, "Actually, it's also called an Australian banyan."

"Okay Miss Botanist," Pua shot back.

"People call it a lot of names, but I call it amazing."

As they admired the tree, Jessica noticed Freddie kind of hunched over and slowly walking toward them, from the alley behind the stores fronting Alii Drive.

Jessica's eyebrows furrowed as Freddie came closer, and she could see he had a black eye. Turning to Pua she said, "Why don't you head over to the pier and I'll catch up with you. I need to talk with Freddie for a couple of minutes."

"Okay, I'll see you in a bit."

Jessica sat on the rock wall under the tree with Freddie. His hair was long dreadlocks and matted from years of having never run a comb through it; his skin was weathered, with a brown, leathery texture. Usually, he had a smile on his face–but not that day.

"What happened to you?" she asked.

Freddie stared at the canoes in the bay as they neared the finish line, but said nothing.

"Who did this to you, was it Bumpy?"

He turned toward her and dipped his chin and turned back toward the bay.

Jessica patted Freddie's leg lightly and said, "He'll never touch you again, I promise."

Jessica went to the pier, found Pua, and they hung out for a couple of hours as they watched the canoe races.

Pua's phone rang, and she glanced at the screen. It was Hiroshi Tamashiro.

"I have to take this," she said, as she stepped back from the crowd watching the races. Jessica nodded.

After a few minutes on the phone, she returned with a big smile.

"Things are looking up. I have to go talk to Mr. Tamashiro later today," she said.

"Great, I'm glad to hear it, I have something I have to go take care of myself." Pua noticed her sister's brows furrowed.

They hugged before Pua left for Lava Java, to get her car, and Jessica went to Emma's Square to find Bumpy.

23

———

After Jessica left the pier, she walked toward Emma's Square to find Bumpy. She sat on the seawall across the street from the plaza and watched him sell drugs while she fought the urge to confront him there.

Instead, she pulled her phone out and dialed retired Detective Grady O'Halleran.

O'Halleran answered on the third ring.

"Hey stranger, it's been a while," a gruff voice said.

"How's retirement? How do you like Kona compared to Honolulu, now that you've been here a while?" Jessica asked.

"I'm fishing at the harbor all the time, what's not to like? My wife and I finally divorced, and I liked it here so much I decided to stay."

"Great–I mean sorry, not the divorce, but..."

O'Halleran interrupted with a laugh. "No worries, I know what you mean."

"Thanks. The reason I'm calling is I remember you had a friend in vice. Is he still there?"

"As far as I know, what's up?"

"A drug dealer, named Bumpy, hangs out at Emma's Square selling dope. Maybe you could ask your friend why

Bumpy hasn't been arrested. It's obvious what he's been up to for some time."

"Emma's Square? Where's that, and what's your interest, if you don't mind my asking?"

"The Square is across from the Palace grounds in the village. My interest is personal."

"So, what do you want to happen with this 'Bumpy' character?"

"I'd like to see him put out of business."

"Okay, I'll make a phone call and see what I can do, and I'll get back to you."

"Thanks, Grady, I owe you one."

After Jessica got off the phone with O'Halleran, she stayed on her side of the street to walk back through the village to get her car at Lava Java. She was almost there when her phone rang. She glanced at the screen and saw it was O'Halleran.

"That was fast."

"Bad news, Bumpy has cousins. Vice has been told he's a low priority and to work on something else every time the subject of Bumpy has been brought up."

"Thanks for trying Grady. We'll take you fishing with us on the boat next time we go."

"Shoots, sounds good."

"Aloha." Next she called Sam but got his voice mail. "Hi honey, Pua and I had a great time this morning. I have something to take care of and I'll be home in a couple of hours or less. I hope you and Henry are having a great time."

Jessica drove to the public parking lot above Emma's Square and parked near the alley entrance. She sat there twenty minutes and watched Bumpy make a couple of deals, then walk toward the alley leading straight toward her.

She got out of her 4Runner and leaned against the front fender as he approached. Bumpy noticed her giving him stink-eye and stopped when he got close to her. "What!" he growled.

"You put lumps on my friend. If you ever touch him again, I'll kick your ass," Jessica said, as she stepped toward Bumpy.

"Oh, I got some of dat for you too sista," he snarled in his local dialect, as he took a swing at her. His fist lightly brushed the side of her face, as she quickly leaned back to get out of the way.

She stepped back, went into her stance and spat, "That's all you got; you punch like a girl. Come on big man, give me your best shot."

Bumpy took another swing, but this time Jessica blocked it and returned an upper cut into the gut. When he grabbed his stomach, and bent over, she followed up with a knee to his nose that broke it. Blood gushed as he was knocked on his ass.

She reached into her truck, grabbed a box of tissue and threw it at Bumpy, as he held his nose trying to stop the blood.

"If there's a next time–you're going to the morgue. I promise."

Bumpy nodded as he took a handful of tissue and held it to his face.

24

———

The house was almost quiet when Jessica got home. Other than Pilau and Mr. Jangles, the cat, nobody was around. "Hi, Mom, the cat did it," Pilau squawked from his perch, when Jessica walked into the living room. "I don't know where he got that from, I didn't teach him that," she thought.

Before she got home, Sam had texted her that he would be down at the boatyard, to check in, and Auntie May and Henry were going to Aloha Village to make leis for the guests.

It was the perfect afternoon to lie on a lounge chair under the shade tree in the backyard. Maybe even take a nap or read a book, or both she thought.

Jessica got comfortable under the tree and read for a while but couldn't get into the story and drifted off to sleep. When she woke up, an hour later, as she sat up and looked out at the bay, she saw a sailboat passing by. It momentarily took her back to a time, more than twenty years earlier when she and Lori Makani survived a nightmare at sea. Most people don't escape serial killers, but Jessica and Lori were among the fortunate.

Still half asleep, she thought about how her life had

worked out so far, and she was content for the most part. But there was something not right with Larry Black that lingered in the back of her mind, and she thought about it from time to time. She had no reason other than a feeling to go on and dismissed it when she heard Sam in the living room talking to Pilau.

"Hi honey," Sam said, as Jessica came into the house. She joined him in front of Pilau's perch and when she hugged him, she looked into his eyes and saw something she hoped she'd never see–his pupils were constricted. She let go and stepped back, thinking for a moment about what she was going to say.

"You look like you saw a ghost," Sam said.

"You have heroin eyes," Jessica said as she stared at Sam.

"I don't know what you're talking about," Sam said as he turned away to go into the kitchen to make coffee.

Jessica followed him, "Tell me you didn't use."

"It's not a big deal; my back was hurting, and I took some medicine to make it go away."

"It is a big deal. What part of "you almost died from it the last time" don't you understand? If you continue taking pain pills, you're going to die of an overdose. You better hope the gardener or someone finds you when that happens, because I won't be here to watch you die. You can smoke weed, you can drink, and you can have more back surgeries. But you can't take any more of those damn drugs."

"Calm down, I got it under control."

Jessica shook her head. "You just don't get it, do you?"

"I can control it this time, don't worry about it," Sam said, as he moved back into the living room while the coffee brewed.

"You better get some Narcan and start carrying it in your shirt pocket with you. Hopefully, someone will know to use it the next time they find you OD'd. I promise you–there will be a next time."

Jessica stormed out of the room to the master bedroom and slammed the door behind her. She went into the closet, pulled her suitcases off the top shelf, opened them up and started filling them with her clothes. When she was finished, she went to Henry's room and packed his clothes, while she wept.

Sam came to the doorway and asked, "What are you doing?"

"I'm leaving and I'm taking Henry with me," she said, as the tears rolled down her cheeks.

You're going to die, and I'm not going to be here to watch it happen."

"Yeah, you've said that about three times."

Jessica stopped packing for a minute and turned to look at Sam. "The only way I would stay is if you would agree to start going to NA meetings every day. But I know you won't because you don't believe you have a problem. When you're ready to quit, let me know–if you live that long."

Sam said, as he watched Jessica packing, "You and Henry can stay, I'll go. Besides, I bought this house for you."

Jessica shook her head, "No, it'll just remind me of you– after you die."

After Jessica had gone, Sam went out to the backyard and sat in the lounge chair Jessica had napped in earlier. "She's wrong," he said to himself. "I can control it." And he popped two pills into his mouth.

❧

Jessica drove out to Aloha Village and picked up Henry, after she explained to Auntie May what was going on.

As she drove along the coastline headed to Pua's apartment, she tried to tell Henry, without crying, they were going to Auntie Pua's house and wouldn't be seeing Sam for a while.

Henry began to cry, and Jessica tried to calm him, as tears streaked down her cheeks. When Pua opened the door and took a look at Jessica holding Henry, she could see on her face something was terribly wrong. She embraced them on the lanai before she invited them in.

"Is Kainoa here?" Jessica asked.

Pua nodded. "Kainoa, come get Henry and show him your room," she yelled. After Henry and Kainoa were out of earshot, Pua asked, "What happened?"

"Sam's using again."

Pua's jaw dropped, "What the–he just got home from rehab. What are you going to do?"

"I don't know, but Henry and I need a place to stay until I can get an apartment."

"You guys can stay here as long as you like. Let's get your things out of the 4Runner."

After they hauled the suitcases upstairs, Pua said, "I have a meeting with Mr. Tamashiro in an hour, so I'm going to start getting ready. You guys make yourselves at home."

"Good luck with that. I hope it works out time for you this time. I'm going to start looking for an apartment while you're gone."

25

Pua met Mr. Tamashiro at her temporary Starbucks office. It was late afternoon and he was on his way into town to have dinner at a new sushi restaurant in the village. She waited for him at her usual table in the corner and had a sweater on when Tamashiro walked in.

"You're cold?"

"It's always cold in here," she said.

He pulled the barstool out from the table and as he sat down, said, "I'm running late for another meeting, so I'll be brief. A long time ago, when I was a young man, I was accused of a serious crime that I didn't have anything to do with. Almost everyone in the small town where I lived thought I did it. The mere accusation destroyed both my business and reputation. Eventually, I was acquitted, but a lot of people still thought I was guilty even though the evidence proved I was innocent.

People are funny that way. But one man, who owned a large business in the same town, gave me a chance and awarded my firm a large contract when no one else would, and the rest is history. I would like you to list the Holualoa property again if you want to."

Pua smiled and, before she could say anything, Tamashiro put his hand out to shake on it. After Tamashiro left, Pua started to work on the MLS listing and by the time she'd had her second espresso, the property was listed for sale online.

Pua would do whatever it took to sell this multimillion dollar estate and wouldn't blow the second chance she'd been given. There was a rumor around town that in one deal, years ago when Kainoa was a toddler, the buyer told her that if she slept with him, he'd make a full price cash offer on her client's property. She was a single parent and had raised her son alone since the boy's father had taken off back to the mainland.

At the time, she thought if lying on her back to close the deal for a hundred and twenty-five thousand dollar commission was what it would take to feed and clothe a special needs child, she had no problem doing the deed.

Before Pua went home she crossed the Starbucks parking lot to L&L Hawaiian Barbecue and ordered a couple of mixed plates with teriyaki chicken and white rice for dinner. That was Jessica's favorite and Pua thought that just might help her feel better after the day she'd had.

She thought about how hard life was back then, as she drove home, and compared it to how she had been feeling the past few months. Times had been hard in the last year because of everything that had happened, but she could see it getting better now that things were starting to go her way again.

When Pua pulled into the driveway at home she heard mariachi music playing next door, and for the first time, in a long while, she felt like dancing.

"How'd it go?" Jessica asked, after Pua walked in the front door carrying a bag with the mixed plate dinners. Pua smiled and said, "I got the listing back on the Holualoa coffee estate, now I just have to sell it." She released a big sigh. "Come on let's eat," she said, with an eager face. "This is going to taste better than anything I've eaten in a long, long time.

26

THREE MONTHS LATER

After a long, hot day Jessica and Gabbie went to the Royal Kona Resort to catch a sunset and have some cool libations to quench their thirst.

They ordered their drinks from the outdoor bar overlooking Kailua Bay. As Jessica and Gabbie waited for the bartender to make their Arnold Palmer's, Jessica noticed Larry Black sitting at the other end of the bar watching the TV mounted above. When he glanced in their direction, he raised his drink in a toast, with his left hand, and went back to watching the evening news report about Erica being indicted for Charles' murder.

After Jessica and Gabbie got their drinks, they wandered over to the shoreline to wait for sunset, and Jessica said, "Have you ever considered maybe Erica wasn't the one who killed Charles, and maybe it was Larry instead?"

"As far as Erica goes, the recording of her cursing at him, with the timestamp near the time of the murder, was good enough for me, and Larry never crossed my mind," Gabbie said.

"It's the 'near the time' that bothers me," Jessica said.

"What makes you think he might have been involved?" Gabbie questioned.

"He's left-handed, just like Erica. Pua said that Charles had poached Larry's client for the big deal she and Charles were working on, that fell through. So, he had motive too. His commission would have been over a million bucks according to Pua."

Jessica glanced in Larry's direction then looked back at Gabbie. "What if he went into Pua's office and finished the job and then framed Erica? It could have been simply a crime of opportunity and once he listened to the recording, he knew he could pin it on her."

Gabbie shifted her eyes from the bright orange sunset toward Jessica, and said, "Do you want to pitch your hypothesis to Erica Black's attorney?"

"Not particularly. It's just a theory, I don't have any proof and I'm not interested in looking for any."

27

Alistair and Hillary Harrington were visiting the Big Island from Santa Barbara. Mrs. Harrington had spent most of their vacation at the Hilton spa every day, and Alistair looking at real estate brochures.

The day before they were to return to Santa Barbara, Mr. Harrington called Pua and asked about touring Tamashiro's coffee estate. "Hi, my wife and I would like to see this property today as we are flying home tomorrow," he said.

"Maybe this is the one, Pua thought," as she grabbed a notepad.

"What time does your flight leave tomorrow?" she asked, ready to jot down the number.

"We fly private and plan to leave about noon. So, we could look at the property as late as tomorrow morning if necessary."

Pua silently mouthed "yes" and fist pumped as she said, "No need, I'll meet you at the estate this afternoon at 3 p.m. if that works for you."

Henry sat at the dining room table chewing on a sausage, as he cut his eyes toward Auntie Pua and smiled at her exuberance, as he continued to chew.

"Yes!" Pua shouted, after she got off the phone, still in her pajamas on the couch. Jessica was in the kitchen making breakfast for Henry and only heard Pua's side of the conversation.

"You have another listing, or something else?"

"Better, a rich couple from the mainland want to see Tamashiro's place this afternoon. Can I borrow your 4Runner? I don't want them to see my old Toyota."

While Jessica flipped pancakes, she said, "Sure. Do you want some pancakes, I still have a couple of Mickey Mouse ones?" she teased.

"No, thanks, I'm too excited. I think I'm going to go for a run to burn off some adrenaline."

Over the previous couple of months, Pua had shown the Tamashiro coffee estate to a couple of "B" list celebrities who didn't have the money, and a lottery winner that made a low ball offer that Mr. Tamashiro declined. This time she felt optimistic it was going to sell.

❦

"I don't know why you would want to buy property here," complained Mrs. Harrington, as she and Mr. Harrington stepped out of the taxi.

"Just wait right here, this won't be long," she demanded of the driver.

The optimism Pua had felt about the older couple melted away as she listened to the woman complain non-stop about the lack of shopping, lack of high society events, and other things she had taken for granted living on the mainland. Pua's optimism was replaced by a sense of doom as she stood and waited to greet the potential buyers.

After a twenty-minute tour of the house, Mrs. Harrington wrinkled her nose, and said, "It smells like mold in here."

"I'm sure that odor can be removed. Let's go look at the

view, it's 180 degrees of the coastline," Pua said, trying to change the subject.

"I doubt it," the fussy woman said, as they passed through the French doors leading to the lanai, that spanned the hundred foot width of the house.

Mr. Harrington didn't say as much, the whole time they were there, as he had on the phone to make the appointment. His hands were cupped together behind his back as they strolled through the main house while his wife complained about anything and everything.

As they stood and looked at the coastline, her final comment was, "Look at the haze, you can hardly see the ocean. And for seventy million, I want to see blue water every time I look out the window. Come on, Alastair, I've seen enough."

Pua sighed as she watched them get into the taxi and leave.

After Pua closed up the house and locked the door, she sat in the truck and called Jessica.

"I need a drink. When I get home, how about we go down to Huggo's and watch the sunset."

"I take it that the showing didn't go well, huh? Gabbie's coming to pick me up, we'll drop Henry off at Auntie May's house and meet you at Huggo's."

A half hour later, Pua met Jessica and Gabbie on the outdoor patio of Huggo's on the Rocks overlooking Kailua Bay.

"Tequila," Pua said to the bartender, before she joined Jessica and Gabbie at a table just above the rocky shoreline. They were mesmerized as they watched a school of tropical fish swim by and hadn't noticed Pua until she pulled out a chair from the table.

Before they could say anything, Pua started with, "Any house up in Holualoa is going to smell like mold if it's been closed up for a while. I tried to explain that to the wife, but she wasn't having any part of it. Needless to say, no offer was made." Pua downed the shot of tequila the waitress had just dropped off. "I probably better switch to wine." Jessica and Gabbie nodded and let Pua vent.

A couple of drinks later, the trio had solved all the world's problems as they watched the sunset. Jessica swore she saw a green flash, Pua and Gabbie weren't so sure as they teased her.

Gabbie's phone chirped, and she looked down to read the text message. "I have to go; I have a date."

Jessica had a confused look on her face. "Date? Spill it girl, you've been holding out on us. Who is this mystery man?"

"Frank Brower," Gabbie said.

Pua and Jessica said, "Uncle Frank? OMG…" in unison.

"I've been seeing him since your wedding. My mother lives in Vegas, so every three months when I go to check on her, we've gotten together. This is the first time he's come to see me here."

"Good for you, he's a nice man," Jessica said, and Pua nodded in agreement.

"And on that note, we have to go home too," Jessica said, as she held her hand out to get the 4Runner keys from Pua.

"It's nice having a built-in designated driver," Pua said, as she handed them over.

❀

Gabbie could never put her finger on it, there was just something about Frank Brower that she couldn't resist. Even though he was 25 years older than her, he had that bad boy mystique about him, since he owned a couple of casinos in Nevada. One of them was in Vegas and the other he was building on the bank of the Colorado River in Laughlin.

She sometimes wondered how he could not have ties to the mob. But after some rudimentary background checking, when she started seeing him, his history came up clean. Why not, she thought, and continued to see him from time to time after she met him at Sam and Jessica's wedding.

It was only about a ten-minute drive from Huggo's to Rays on the Bay, at the Keauhou Sheraton, where Frank was staying. There was no missing him, as he sat at the table in the restaurant waiting for Gabbie. He looked like an older version of Clark Gable, and he always wore a Tommy Bahama shirt wherever he went.

"I'm sorry I'm late. Traffic was backed up on Alii Drive, somebody ran over a jogger and the road was closed while the cops investigated. So, I had to double back and go around the long way to get here.

"You look beautiful as ever," he said, as he stood and kissed her, before he scooted her chair in as she sat down.

"Are you still looking for property to buy here?" Gabbie asked.

Frank nodded as he waved to the waitress that they were ready.

Gabbie continued, "Pua has a large coffee estate she's trying to sell."

Gabbie went on to tell him about the particulars of the property as had been related to her from Pua.

"I could use a big write-off; I want to see it. I'll call her tomorrow," Frank said, as his eyes twinkled at the prospect for seeing Gabbie more often.

28

Sam came to and his mind was fuzzy. His head was throbbing just like it had every morning for the past few months. His "go to move" every morning had been to grab the bottle of Vicodin on his nightstand and take three or four to get right with the world. Just as Jessica had predicted, Sam had become a slave to the pills, and he could no longer control how many of them he took per day.

Still in a daze, he rolled over on his side and expected Jessica to be there. Once his eyes focused, he cut them toward their family portrait on the nightstand. He, Jessica, and Henry, they looked so happy. He thought about how he had so messed that up.

Next to the framed portrait was a plaque that said, "*A house is only a home when there is love present.*"

He reached over and grabbed it. Re-reading the text his eyes began to water and he hurled the plaque against the wall.

When Jessica left and took Henry with her, Sam had no idea the amount of emotional pain he was in for. Most of the time the pills dampened it. But they'd quit working and the stark reality that he'd screwed up his marriage confronted him every morning, and he was sick of it. He missed being Henry's dad and Jessica wouldn't allow him to be alone with Henry under any circumstances.

The house had become only a place he passed out in every night and the love had left it the day Jessica took Henry and walked out. Sam's daily existence now revolved around getting more pills. He tried to regulate how many he took per day, but it was futile–the pills had taken over.

"Maybe she's right, maybe I'll die from this if I don't get it under control," he thought. In recent weeks, every morning he said he wasn't going to take any more pills but every day he lost the battle of choice when his addiction demanded he swallow just one more. Over and over the cycle repeated itself and at that point Sam was no longer in control.

For the first time, Sam came to the conclusion that there was no way he was going to beat the monster within on his own. He decided his life needed to change before it was too late. He looked up the phone number for Narcotics Anonymous and dialed the number. A man on the other end of the line asked him, "Do you think you have a problem?"

"I'm way past that, when's the next meeting and where is it?" Sam asked.

"There's a meeting tonight at the Big Game Fishing Club out at the harbor," the man said.

"There's no way I'll stay sober that long. How about an AA meeting sooner?"

"I know there's a meeting at the Stone Church on Alii Drive this morning. Do you need someone to give you a ride?"

"No, I can make it on my own. Thanks," Sam said and hung up the phone.

"All I want to do God, is make it to that meeting. Think you can help me out?" Sam prayed, as he glanced at the clock and saw he'd have to hurry to make it to the meeting on time.

When Sam arrived at the church, the parking lot was full, and he had to park down the street. The voice in his head was out to get him that morning. And as he looked for a place to park, he thought, "See, no parking, you should just go home," the first voice said. As his mind struggled, a second, inner voice, shouted, "Shut up and park the car. You certainly would walk a little for more Vicodin, you can walk to stay sober." After contemplating which voice was the right one, he went with the latter and parked the car.

The last thing he expected to see when he finally got to the meeting was anyone he knew. Sam sat in the back of the group, bent over with his head in his hands, and just tried to listen to people share. The meeting was outdoors on the church lawn, next to the ocean. That morning the surf was booming as the waves broke against the rocky shoreline. It was hard for Sam to hear but for some unknown reason he felt a sense of hope for the first time.

After thirty minutes Sam started to get up and leave before the meeting was over, when he looked across the group of people and saw who he least expected–Uncle Frank and Jessica. They weren't looking in his direction, so he quickly sat back down before they saw him.

He wanted to avoid a conversation with them that morning. He needed to see if he could not take any more pills that day, so he could make it to the NA meeting that night. Five minutes before the meeting was over, he saw Uncle Frank and Jessica leave the meeting. Sam felt a sigh of relief that he wouldn't have to talk to them–especially his uncle.

After the meeting Sam didn't hang around to talk to anyone and went straight to his car. Leaning against the side of the car, waiting for him, was his worst fear, Uncle Frank.

"Have you had enough yet?" he asked, in a gruff tone.

Sam nodded, as he looked down, his eyes filled with despair.

29

U ncle Frank and Gabbie met Pua at the front gates of the Tamashiro coffee estate, in Holualoa, at 10 a.m. For once in her life, she arrived early, and the tour of the property got off to a good start.

Unlike the last time Pua showed the estate, Gabbie was the significant other and continuously talked up the property, instead of complaining about everything like Mrs. Harrington.

That morning the Kona winds had blown the volcanic haze that normally engulfed the coastline toward Oahu. As a result, the views were spectacular, with the sky and ocean deep blue and the island of Maui visible in the distance.

After touring the guest bungalow, the trio went to see the main house. Pua said, as they walked through the house, "You can see koa wood has been used throughout the home for floors and cabinets. No expense was spared during construction."

Uncle Frank nodded in agreement as he looked around the house at all the custom built-ins, and said, "The Japanese carpentry is as fine as any I've ever seen. Whoever built this house was a real craftsman. I've almost seen enough, let's go check out the view," as he headed toward the French doors leading to the lanai.

Uncle Frank admired the view as he stood on the lanai with his hands on the rail, scanning the 180-degree views of the coastline.

"Uncle Frank's Kona Coffee has a nice ring to it," Gabbie said, as they studied the ninety-acre coffee orchard below the lanai. Uncle Frank nodded, turned to Pua, and said, "Let's make an offer."

Gabbie wondered for a moment what "let's" really meant and then dismissed it as she was overthinking their relationship.

That afternoon Pua called Mr. Tamashiro and told him she had a cash offer. "I'm coming to town later, I'll meet you at the same Starbucks as the last time at 2 p.m., if that works for you," he said.

"Of course, I'll see you then."

Pua had imagined the moment many times and thought more than once how it might never happen.

She was at her usual corner table in the back when Tamashiro arrived. This time he wasn't rushing and ordered a latte before he sat down with her.

"Like I said earlier on the phone, it's not a full price offer, but it's close and it's a thirty-day escrow," Pua said. A slight nervousness in her voice.

Tamashiro nodded, pulled out his glasses and began to read the offer, as the barista handed Pua a latte over the nearby counter. Tamashiro sipped it as he continued to read all the details of the proposed offer. After he sat the paper down on the table, he hesitated to say anything for a minute and took another sip before he answered. Pua's gut was tied up in a knot until he said, "It's a deal–you did a good job, Pua."

She thanked him for giving her another chance and said that she was truly grateful. After he left, she sat there and was overwhelmed with emotion by the magnitude of what had happened in her life since the false tsunami warning. Charles had stolen a hundred and fifty thousand dollars from her company that she had to pay back to rental clients. After he was murdered, she was arrested for it and had to stand trial. She'd lost her home, was emotionally and financially bank-rupt and had to move into an apartment that had rats in the ceiling. She lost the biggest real estate deal of her career, then she got it back when she needed it most. She recalled the hell of the past year and a half while she sipped an iced tea–tears streamed down her cheeks. She wanted to ugly cry so bad, but held it together because people were starting to stare.

"Are you okay," asked one of the baristas that she had come to know during her daily visits. Pua nodded as she wiped the tears away. "I'm more than okay, I'm just fine, thanks."

That evening Pua, Jessica, Henry, and Kainoa met Uncle Frank and Gabbie at the Kona Inn for a celebratory dinner. Soft, modern slack-key guitar melodies drifted through the restaurant as they made their way to a private banquet table.

After they were seated, Uncle Frank said, "I love the antique fans here," as he looked up at them mounted on the ceiling, with their interconnected belt-drive system, to a single electric motor. "How old is place, does anybody know?"

Jessica volunteered, "If I recall correctly it was built in the twenties; the inn was for the first visitors brought to the island via steamship."

After dinner, as Kainoa and Henry played on the sea wall, the adults had coffee and dessert and talked story. Uncle Frank said he had an announcement before the last drink and the last bite of mud pie were gone.

He stood and said, "That new coffee farm I bought today is too big for just one person to live on." He turned his eyes toward Gabbie, reached into his pocket and pulled out a ring box. Gabbie, Pua and Jessica all gasped in unison.

"I'd get down on one knee, but I might not be able to get back up," he said, half joking as he opened the ring box. Jessica and Pua laughed, but quickly covered their mouths while Gabbie had that deer-in-the-headlights look as she stared at the three-carat diamond engagement ring.

Gabbie got up from her chair and wrapped her arms around Uncle Frank's neck, shook her head, then held out her left hand for him to slip the ring on.

30

"I'm tired of us having rats for roommates. Let's go look at houses today," Pua said, as she and Jessica sat at the kitchen table having their morning coffee together.

"Amen," Jessica said, before she took another sip of coffee.

Later that day, they'd walked through half a dozen houses and were in the last one Pua wanted to see. It was a repo, in rough shape, but had a great ocean view. Pua pointed and said, "What do you think that stain on the wall is?"

"Probably blood from the scene of the crime," Jessica said, causing them both to laugh as Jessica's phone rang.

"Hey Uncle, what's up?" she said as she and Pua stood in the living room of the vacant house.

"I've been going to NA meetings with Sam the last couple of weeks trying to help him get some time under his belt. He's got about fourteen days of sobriety. He was hoping you might let him see Henry before he travels with me to the mainland."

"You're going to the mainland, what about the wedding, and why is Sam going with you?" Jessica said, in rapid succession.

"I told Gabbie this morning we have to postpone it until I get back, or we can meet in Vegas and get married there."

Jessica paused for a minute, "As far as Sam seeing Henry, I'll think about it and let you know later. And if he starts getting any ideas of getting back together, because he's been sober more than fifteen minutes, you can tell him I won't even entertain the thought of having anything to do with him until he can stay clean for at least a year."

"Deal."

After Jessica put her phone back in her purse, Pua asked, "What was that all about?"

"That was Uncle Frank; he said Sam's been clean for about two weeks and is going to meetings."

Pua sighed, "It's about time the black cloud that's been hanging over our ohana took a break."

As they stepped out to the lanai, to see the view, Jessica said, "You got that right. I hope he makes it, but I'm prepared for the worst. I've seen too many people die from opiate overdoses. If there really is a God, it's time for him, it, or she to step up to the plate."

Pua turned, gave a long look, and said, "Who do you think sent Uncle Frank?"

"Since when did you get religion?"

"Since I lost all of my shit and almost went to prison. I don't know, it just looks like a pretty clear sign to me that something is working in Sam's life."

Jessica nodded, "Maybe you're right, we'll see."

Pua opened the front door and said,

"I've seen enough of this dump, let's go to Starbucks, they're probably wondering where I've been."

While they were headed to Starbucks, Jessica texted

Gabbie and asked if she'd like to join them. Gabbie texted back a few minutes later, "On my way."

All the regulars waved and nodded to Pua as she and Jessica came in the front door. Pua grabbed her regular table in the back corner. It was almost always vacant because most people avoided sitting there due to the fact it was always cold enough to hang meat in that part of the room. Pua had told the manager more than once it was too cold, and he always replied there was nothing he could do about it since the temperature was controlled from a central location.

After Pua grabbed their lattes that were waiting for them off of the counter, she said, "Are you and Gabbie still going to do private investigations after the dust settles in everyone's life?"

"No. After the first job of following Erica around trying to get photos of her and Charles together, I decided life was too short to do work I didn't like anymore. I've been thinking about starting a tour boat business. I have to get back to spending a lot more time on the ocean, and it would be good for Henry, too."

When Gabbie walked in the front door, she didn't take off her sunglasses, which piqued Jessica's curiosity. After Gabbie had ordered her drink and came to the table, she still had them on. Jessica asked, "Have you been crying?"

Gabbie nodded and pulled a tissue out of her purse to wipe her nose.

"Frank's sick. He told us last night he had to go back to the mainland in a few days because he had business to take care of. He just left out the part that it's for chemo and radiation. I checked his text messages when he was in the bathroom, you know, an old habit from when I was married to that cheating bastard Karl, years ago. When I saw the female doctor's name, I had to read it. I thought it was just some woman who'd texted him at first. Of course, I confronted him and asked him why he didn't tell me."

"That's why Sam's going with him," Jessica said.

Gabbie nodded and continued, "The plan is Sam's going so he can help him through it, and then they're going to come back to Kona. I offered to go and take care of him, but he said, 'no way' because he didn't want me to think that's why he asked me to marry him."

Jessica nodded and said, "I'll be back in a minute," then stepped outside to call Uncle Frank.

31

———

When Jessica had called Uncle Frank earlier, she said Sam could come to the apartment that evening and see Henry while he was asleep. They both agreed it would be less traumatic for everyone and the best thing to do.

Kainoa was away on an overnight fishing trip with Uncle Jack so Henry was alone in the bedroom they shared. Sam sat in the room and watched the boy as he slept, while he lightly stroked his hair, careful not to wake him.

After he came out of the bedroom, Pua went to hers so Sam and Jessica could have some privacy.

"You look good, keep doing what you're doing, it's working," Jessica said.

"I love you," Sam replied, as his eyes welled.

Jessica nodded but didn't respond as she opened the front door for him to leave. The tears rolled down her face as she stood there quiet.

Sam stepped outside the door and turned, and she said, "I love you, but I can't be with you until after you take care of yourself." She closed the door and slid down the face of it to the floor, where she sat and cried, until Pua came out of her room. Pua sat down on the floor next to her sister and put her arm around her and just let her cry.

⁂

S am met Uncle Frank at the Kona Airport at 6 a.m. for the flight to Laughlin, Nevada.

"You have to give me the number of the guy that painted 'Jessica' on your plane," Uncle Frank said, as they drove past Sam's Gulfstream jet parked on the ramp.

"I think Gabbie would like it if I put her name on mine, or, soon to be ours."

"Sure," Sam said as he nursed a large cup of coffee.

"We should arrive early enough to have dinner, and then we can hit the eight o'clock meeting over in Bullhead."

Six hours later they landed in Bullhead City, Arizona and caught a ride to the water taxi on the Arizona side of the Colorado River.

Uncle Frank pointed south as they boarded the pontoon boat, and said, "Construction of my resort down river is mired in red tape with the state, so it doesn't look like I'll be moving out of the Riverside Hotel anytime soon. I've arranged for you to have the suite right next to mine."

Sam shifted his eyes toward Uncle Frank, and said, "Is that so I can be close if you need help or just to keep an eye on me?"

"Both," Uncle Frank said, just before he spit in the river and put a cigarette in his mouth. While he fumbled for his lighter, he continued, "We're both going to need each other and it's not going to be easy for either of us. My doctor said the chemo and radiation are going to knock my dick in the dirt and I'm going to need some help afterward. And you are nowhere near being out of the woods as far staying clean goes."

The pontoon boat docked on the Nevada side of the river and Sam and Uncle Frank slowly walked up the ramp to the entrance of the hotel. When Sam pulled open the glass door leading into the casino, he was almost bowled over by the stench of cigarette smoke that hit him in the face. It was no wonder to him why his uncle had cancer, between a lifetime of smoking and hanging out in casinos, he was surprised his uncle had lived as long as he had.

"I love Hawaii, but you can't get an open-faced turkey sandwich in Kona like they have here," Uncle Frank said as they sat down in the café at a table next to the glass wall that overlooked the river.

"Or cancer either when going out to eat," Sam thought.

❀

The next day, after they went to the morning AA meeting across the river in Bullhead, Sam drove Uncle Frank to his doctor in Kingman, about thirty-five miles from Laughlin.

"I doubt I'll ever understand why you like this place," Sam said as they drove through the desert.

"There's beauty here, it's just a different color, brown, and I happen to like brown. The clear blue sky, the clean air and the genuine people that live in the area. There are a lot of snakes here, but they aren't of the two-legged variety that seems to be prevalent in a lot of other places."

"I guess if brown is your favorite color then this is the place. Aren't there any doctors in Bullhead that you like? Why all the way to Kingman?"

"The medical center in Kingman is tied in with the Mayo Clinic. And while it's thirty-five miles, it goes by fast because there's no traffic like there is in the cities, take Vegas for example," Uncle Frank replied.

Sam had noticed Uncle Frank had been limping for over a month and that was the reason he was going to the doctor.

While Uncle Frank was waiting to see the doctor, Sam went across the street from the office to an In-N-Out Burger stand and got a double-double with cheese. It was the one true thing he did miss from the mainland. He liked the mushroom Swiss burger at Quinn's in Kona, but it just wasn't the same thing as In-N-Out.

When Uncle Frank came out of the doctor's office, he didn't look happy. The last time Sam remembered his uncle looking like that was at the funeral of his parents.

"I'm sorry, I couldn't wait to eat. You want to get a burger before going back to Laughlin?"

Uncle Frank shook his head.

The drive across the desert was too quiet for Sam, and he finally asked, "What did the doctor say?"

Uncle Frank stared out of the passenger side window at the desert and said, "Nothing good."

A month had passed, and Uncle Frank still hadn't told Sam what the doctor in Kingman had said the first time Sam had driven him there. And during that month, they had spent all of their time going to AA meetings and doctor appointments in Kingman. It took two weeks before Uncle Frank finally leveled with Sam, as they drove across the desert, headed to Kingman.

"The limp is caused by bone cancer. There's an excellent chance I'm not going to beat it."

Most of the time Uncle Frank had joked about some hard spots he'd been in during his life. But this time he was serious because he knew it was likely there wasn't going to be any looking back years later at how he had survived cancer.

"I'm sorry. If there's anything you want, I'll get it," Sam said.

"Yes, stop at the new marijuana dispensary when we get back to Laughlin."

Sam had a grim look on his face. "Are you sure?"

Uncle Frank shook his head, "Don't worry, I was never a pothead. It's the only way I'm ever going to eat again. Now if I tell you to stop at the liquor store for a bottle of Wild Turkey, feel free to ignore that."

Uncle Frank had good days and bad, it depended on when he had chemotherapy.

The day escrow was scheduled to close, on the Holualoa coffee estate, was a day Uncle Frank felt awful from the chemo. Sam had to bring a wheelchair with them to the bank so his uncle could make the wire transfer. Uncle Frank could hardly walk more than a few steps anymore from the pain in his leg.

As they drove back to the hotel, Uncle Frank said, "If it wasn't for Gabbie, I doubt I'd continue treatment, that's how bad I feel. She's the only thing that keeps me going right now. Well, that and living long enough to see you get a one-year chip for sobriety. Otherwise, I'd just off myself now and be done with it."

Sam processed those words and realized he now needed to be strong enough for the both of them.

32

———————

After the wire transfer had been completed, the escrow officer at the title company called Pua and asked if she'd like her commission direct deposited or paid by check. "Oh, I want the check, so I can take a photo of it," she said, as she grinned.

After Pua had picked up her check, she sat in her car holding the envelope that held the piece of paper that was going to free her from driving an old car and having rats in the ceiling. She looked both directions before opening it, as if someone might want to take it from her. "Hmm, maybe I should have done direct deposit," she thought for a second before finally looking inside the envelope.

Her heart raced as she read the dollar amount printed on the check. When she saw $2,091,000 printed on it, a sigh of relief washed over her as she stuffed it in her purse and called Jessica.

"Can you come and get me? And bring your gun? I need an escort to the bank," Pua joked. Her heart pounded at ninety beats a minute. "Of course, I was just kidding about the gun. But I do need a ride to the car dealer after I make the deposit, and to drop off my car at that place up mauka that takes vehicle donations."

"Where are you going to buy a new car from?" Jessica asked.

"I'm not buying new, since I've had humility stomped into me one nickel at a time. Since Charles and the trial, I'm going to get something pre-owned but only a year or two old. And tomorrow I'm going to buy a house."

"Please, tell me it's not the one with the possible murder scene on the wall," Jessica teased.

"No, there's a house across from the bay at Kahaluu. It's perfect for what I want, and it's big enough for all of us. I'll just walk across the street and be at the beach. I'm going to start training for Ironman again and being able to walk out the door, just steps to the ocean, will be awesome."

Thirty minutes later, Jessica picked up Pua standing out in front of the credit union in Kainaliu. Pua had donated the car and deposited the escrow check. Now it was time to head back down the hill to the car lot and buy a 4Runner that she'd had her eye on for the last week. It looked like new, was only a year old, and Pua was perfectly happy to let someone else take the depreciation hit for the pleasure of driving it off the lot when it was new.

It was a perfect afternoon as they drove down the hill into Kona. The sky was clear, and the temperature was eighty-five degrees with light trade winds.

Jessica and Pua were excited and talking about all the possibilities of moving across from the beach park when the news on the radio came on and the announcer said, "Erica Black has just been acquitted on all charges in the death of Charles Lim." They quit talking for a moment, then Pua reached over and turned the radio off.

"What the hell? Why didn't the jury convict her?" Pua said.

Jessica kept her eyes on the road and said, "You probably aren't going to want to hear this, but I don't think she did it."

Pua slumped in her seat, put her hand to her forehead for a moment and shook her head.

"As long as they don't start looking at me again…"

"Don't worry, they won't. The judge dismissed your case with prejudice, and they can't file murder charges against you again."

33

———————

THREE WEEKS LATER

"I tell you what, I'm going to see this new doctor that just arrived in Kingman, and if he can't come up with a game plan to make me feel better than hammered dog shit, I'm going to make a trip to one of those states with legal suicide and check out permanently. I'm gonna die, now it's just a matter of when and how. But I'll be damned if I let the cancer torture my ass to the end."

Uncle Frank and Sam made the weekly drive to Kingman, but this time to see the new doctor in the oncology unit. He was a young guy, fresh from Johns Hopkins Hospital in Baltimore.

As they drove across the desert, Uncle Frank told Sam about this new doctor and how he had high hopes that maybe he knew something the other doctor he'd been seeing didn't.

It was fifteen minutes past the time for his appointment, and Uncle Frank was frustrated and anxious to meet his physician. He sighed as he turned to Sam, and grumbled, "I'm starting to not like this new MD."

An old guy, sitting across from Frank, couldn't help but overhear his comment. The man grinned and said, "I've met him once, he's a nice kid. I think he comes here after he throws his paper route."

Uncle Frank just shook his head and sighed again.

Ten more minutes had passed when a nurse stuck her head into the waiting room and called Uncle Frank's name.

"Well, let's go see Doogie Howser," he said gruffly, as he looked at Sam.

Sam pushed his uncle's wheelchair down the hall, as they followed the nurse to a small room. They sat in there and waited another five minutes before Dr. Richardson came in.

He was young, very young, just like the man in the waiting room had said. Uncle Frank had been sober a long time and the one thing he'd learned, during that period of time, was to keep his mouth shut more often than not. On that particular day, he was fresh out of restraint and said,

"Do your parents know where you are?"

Dr. Richardson glanced at his watch and fired right back, "About right now, they probably think I just got out of school, and I'm about to start my paper route. Which is usually right, but today I got a substitute for the route, so I could come down here and meet with you."

Uncle Frank admired the kid's quick wit and sense of humor. He smiled and toned down his attitude from then on.

"But seriously, I've reviewed your case and I have some good news, Mr. Brower. There's a new experimental drug out on the market that we're going to try and treat you with, if you're game."

Uncle Frank raised an eyebrow. "It's the 'if I'm game' part that scares me. I hope it has whiskey in it, preferably Wild Turkey."

"No, it doesn't have whiskey in it. But if this doesn't work, we'll get you a bottle of Wild Turkey if that'll make you feel better."

"Well, let's try this miracle cure first," Uncle Frank said.

As Sam and Uncle Frank drove back to Laughlin, Sam

said, "While you were busy insulting him, I googled Dr. Richardson. It turns out he's some kind of super genius who graduated from college at age 14 and then went to medical school."

"No shit?" Uncle Frank said as he pulled his pack of cigarettes out of his shirt pocket.

"Yeah, according to what I read online, he's got more smarts in his little finger than both of us put together."

Uncle Frank cracked his window, lit a cigarette and said, "I hope so, because otherwise I'm chop suey," as he blew smoke out the window.

❦

For the next seven days, Uncle Frank took the experimental medication every morning and when he went to see Dr. Richardson the following week, he looked like a whole new man. The amazing part was he didn't even need the wheelchair anymore.

When Dr. Richardson entered the room, he looked at his patient and joked, "Wow, that stuff actually worked."

"Dr. Richardson, I'm sorry I gave you such a hard time when we first met. But this new medication that you've given me has made a one hundred percent improvement in the way I feel. At this point, if I die and I still feel this good, I'm okay with that."

Sam and Uncle Frank stayed in Laughlin for another three months and every week they made the trip to Kingman to see Dr. Richardson until it was time for Uncle Frank to get a PET scan.

His uncle's progress had been so good, now Sam just waited in the car for him, while he chowed down on a couple of In-N-Out cheeseburgers, every trip. When Uncle Frank came out, to get back in the car this time, he had that something-wasn't-good look again, "What did the doctor say about your PET Scan?"

Uncle Frank sighed, "He said it looks like a Christmas tree."

"What does that mean?"

"It means it's time to go back to Kona."

"But you look great... I don't get it."

"Yeah, my body is rallying right now, but the PET scan says I better get my affairs in order–sooner than later. I want to believe that it's going to be okay, but I've been around a long time. Granted I'm no doctor, but I've known people with cancer and I've seen this happen, where the person was on death's doorstep, and then they look like they're going to recover, then boom, the cancer returns with a vengeance, and they go paws up." He snapped his fingers. "Just like that."

"I'm sorry uncle. When we get back to the hotel, I'll make the arrangements for the plane."

Until the results of the PET scan came back, Uncle Frank felt like he'd finally turned the corner in his treatment and thought he might be the exception to the rule and beat the cancer that had ravaged his body.

He sat looking out the window of his hotel suite, over-looking the Colorado River. Coffee cup in one hand, and cigarette in the other, he watched the water taxi go back and forth to the Arizona side of the river to pick up hotel employees who had parked their vehicles in the employee parking lot there.

Sam popped his head into the room and said, "I'm ready if you are?" Uncle Frank took another drag off his cigarette and nodded.

When Uncle Frank's Gulfstream jet landed at Bullhead

City, and taxied to the terminal, it was the first time he'd seen it since he had Gabbie's name painted on the side of it.

He smiled and said, "It looks good, I hope she likes it."

Sam smiled and tried not to think about how it reminded him of Jessica.

34

"Last night, when I talked to Frank on the phone, he said his cancer treatment is working, he says it's in remission."

"That's great to hear," Jessica said, as she put her arm around Gabbie and hugged as she parked the 4Runner.

"He and Sam will be back on the island soon," Gabbie said, as she and Jessica walked down the sandy path toward the little beach at the end of the runway of the Old Kona Airport.

When they got to the edge of the small crescent beach, they took off their shoes and walked down to the water's edge as small waves lapped at the shoreline. They wiggled and dug their toes into the sand as warm seawater washed over their feet.

"This place is perfect. I loved it so much when you and Sam got married here. I appreciate you giving Frank and me your blessing to have ours here, too."

Jessica nodded and said, "Have you heard Erica Black was found not guilty?"

"I did." Gabbie cracked a grin, "I also heard her lawyer had miraculously come up with a theory of how Larry did it and was so convincing at closing that the jury found Erica innocent in less than four hours."

"Oh really," Jessica said.

"I detect sarcasm," Gabbie said as she smiled.

Again, Jessica changed the subject, "I thought you guys were going to wait a little longer before getting married?"

"We don't have time. His cancer seems to be in remission, and we want to get on with the business of living together… as much as we can."

As they walked back and forth in the surf, Jessica couldn't contain her curiosity anymore and asked, "Do you know how Sam's doing?"

Gabbie looked surprised, "I thought you said once upon a time that topic was off-limits."

"I can't help it. I look around here and everything I see reminds me of him–everything." Jessica pointed at a couple of big lava rocks on the beach. "We leaned against them for one of our wedding photos." She turned and pointed the opposite direction and said, "We took sunset photos there," as she looked to the west. "Behind us was where we took the group photo that everyone was in."

Gabbie nodded, "I remember," and she grabbed Jessica's hand. "Frank says he thinks Sam has a good shot at making it this time. He says his attitude is different from the first time, and that he wants to stay clean. He's doing this for himself instead of being forced to."

Jessica nodded as she wiped away a tear that had rolled down her cheek.

As they were walking back to Jessica's 4Runner, Gabbie got a text that said Uncle Frank and Sam were an hour out of Kona.

"Speaking of the devils, can you take me home so I can get my car to go pick them up?" Gabbie said.

Jessica didn't answer right away and Gabbie started to repeat herself, when Jessica said, "I'm sorry, I heard you the first time. I was just thinking for a minute that maybe we could go out to Aloha Village and get Henry, and then we could go together…"

"I thought you wouldn't have anything to do with Sam until he'd been clean for a year?"

"Yeah, I said that. But I think it's time I meet him halfway–and Henry needs him."

❦

Gabbie and Jessica drove out to Aloha Village and picked up Henry. Jessica glanced into the back seat where Henry was strapped in, and said, "We can fit two more people back there, don't ya think?" Henry smiled and nodded, while he played his Game Boy.

The drive from Aloha Village was not far and a short time later, they'd arrived at the airport, before Uncle Frank and Sam's plane landed. The women sat there and talked about having the wedding reception at the coffee estate, while they waited for the plane to arrive.

It wasn't long before the plane landed and taxied to a parking spot where Gabbie and Jessica could see it.

Jessica saw the moment Gabbie recognized her name had been painted on the side of the jet. It was obvious because her mouth hung wide open as she gawked at it.

"Oh, he's got it bad girl," Jessica said as she smiled.

Gabbie beamed, leaned near Jessica and whispered so Henry couldn't hear, "Yes, he does. I'm gonna rock his world later if he's up for it."

They sat and waited while the shuttle van from Air Services drove out to the plane, to retrieve the two men, and bring them back to the parking lot.

Henry had been playing a game and not really paying attention to what was happening, until he looked up and saw

Sam and Uncle Frank getting out of the shuttle van in front of the Air Services office across the parking lot.

"I want to see Sam; I want to see Sam!" he yelled excitedly.

"Okay, okay, we'll see Sam, just hang on a minute."

The women got out of the vehicle and Gabbie went to Uncle Frank, while Jessica got Henry out of the back seat.

Sam saw Henry and started walking faster and faster toward the 4Runner, as Jessica held Henry's hand. She wanted to let him run to Sam but there was a vehicle between them pulling into a parking spot, so she held his hand tight until the vehicle was stopped.

By then Sam was only twenty or thirty feet away and Jessica let go of Henry's hand. The boy ran his little feet as fast as he could toward Sam, who picked him up and swung him around as he hugged him tightly.

Jessica stood back and let Sam and Henry get reacquainted. As Sam took a knee to be eye level with Henry, he brushed the tears from his eyes a couple of times as he talked to him, while Jessica watched from a few feet away.

Sam looked up at her and mouthed, "Thank you."

"Okay Henry, time to get back in the truck," Jessica said.

Sam picked him up and carried him to the vehicle and put him in the back seat.

Sam and Jessica stepped away from the vehicle, out of earshot from Henry, and she embraced him for the first time since she'd taken Henry and left him.

"Henry and I will come home when you get your one-year chip."

"I will get it, I know I'm not supposed to promise, but if I keep doing what I'm doing, I'll get it."

As Jessica nodded, Sam said, "I have to go help uncle."

Everyone hesitated when it came time to get into the 4Runner because they were unsure where they each should sit. Sam didn't want Jessica to think he was pushing by automatically hopping in the front seat next to her or even acting like he should drive. Gabbie finally broke the tension and took charge. "You're driving," as she looked at Jessica. "You're sitting shotgun, pointing to Sam, and the rest of us will get in the back with Henry." Everyone nodded, did as instructed and were happy there was no further drama.

After Jessica dropped everyone off at the coffee estate, in Holualoa, she and Henry went to their new home for the time being. It was just north of Kahaluu Beach Park and in walking distance to some of the best snorkeling in the world.

Later that afternoon, Jessica and Pua sat on the lanai watching the sun set over Kahaluu Bay. "I don't know what the hell got into me. Gabbie and I were at the beach where Sam and I got married, and the next thing I know I'm telling him we're coming home when he gets his one-year chip."

"Iron Jessica melted huh?" Pua said, as she smiled.

"Like ice cream in July."

35

I t was five thirty in the morning when Jessica awoke. She
hadn't slept much the night before. Between the loud surf
and Sam, she woke up a half a dozen times during the night
thinking about him. She wanted to go home, but knew it was
too soon. Sam had enough on his plate with going to meetings and being Uncle Frank's caretaker.

Henry and Kainoa were still asleep. Pua had gotten up,
turned the coffee on, and was getting ready to go for a swim.
She had started training hard for the Ironman triathlon and
was swimming two and a half miles every morning before
going to Starbucks.

Jessica got a cup of coffee and went out on the lanai to
watch the waves across the street. It was still peaceful outside
even though Alii Drive ran past the front of the house. Most
people wouldn't leave for work for another hour or so. As she
sipped her coffee, she heard doves cooing and the sound of
wild parrots squawking as they flew overhead.

The peaceful tranquility was obliterated when two police
SUVs raced by, as she took another sip of coffee. They were
followed a few minutes later by an ambulance, with lights
flashing, but no siren.

Seconds later, it was quiet again, like nothing had ever happened to disturb the tranquility. But she could see the emergency lights flashing down the street in the Kahaluu Beach parking lot. The ambulance had left a few minutes after it arrived with no emergency lights. "Hopefully nothing bad happened," she thought, as she got up and went back inside the house to get ready to go meet Gabbie at Starbucks later that morning.

Before Jessica left the house, Auntie May stopped by to pick up Henry just as she had every week since Sam and Jessica adopted him. Henry loved going to Aloha Village with her, so he could play with auntie's boys and the other kids there, visiting the island with their parents. Auntie May had told Jessica more than once that Henry was their best lei maker in his age group, and the unofficial children's ambassador of the resort.

It had been an hour and a half since the police and ambulance had gone past the house and Jessica was surprised to see the police still down the street, as she drove by on her way to meet Gabbie.

"So much for I hope nothing bad happened," she thought, as she passed the crime scene that had been taped off in a corner of the parking lot. She knew from experience anytime the police were on scene more than an hour, and there was crime scene tape, there was a good chance somebody got murdered. She did a quick calculation in her head and thought it was about time for the annual murder. There hadn't been one in town since Charles Lim.

The rest of Jessica's drive to town was uneventful, and she didn't think anything more about the police activity at the park. It was a typical day in Kona, and the weather was about like it had been, most of the time, in the previous eighty thousand years.

Gabbie had arrived first and sat outside of Starbucks on

the lanai. "You aren't going to believe this," Gabbie said, as Jessica sat down with her coffee.

"What?"

"Larry Black was arrested this morning. I heard it on the news on the way down here."

Jessica's brow furrowed, and she said, "For Charles Lim's murder?"

"No, they said he killed his wife, Erica. Apparently, he dumped her body at Kahaluu Beach Park, and somebody got his license plate and called it in."

"Wow, I didn't see that coming. I thought maybe the DA would try and sign him up for Charles' murder, and they might still. But I guess the thought of Erica getting a lot of his money in a divorce was too much for him."

Gabbie stirred a couple tablespoons of sugar into her coffee as Jessica's face wrinkled as she watched.

"I still don't know how you drink it like that."

Gabbie smiled, "So how's Henry after seeing Sam? And, how are you?"

"Surprisingly he was okay after I dropped you guys off yesterday. And I'm okay." Gabbie smiled, but she didn't ask anymore because she didn't want to pry.

Then Jessica offered, "Did Sam say anything to you about the conversation I had with him yesterday?"

Gabbie shook her head. "He just talked about being glad to be back on the island. I thought he was never going to shut up last night so Frank and I could go to bed."

"How is Uncle Frank doing?"

"He looks like he's doing okay, but he's cagey about the details of what's going on with him. Other than the doctor has him on some new medicine, getting information out of that guy is like trying to get gold out of Fort Knox. The only thing he was forthcoming about was he wants to have the ceremony in the next couple of weeks, so that's the plan. Two weeks from now we'll have the wedding on the beach and then the reception at the coffee estate."

"Two Saturdays from now is perfect timing because this Saturday Pua is competing in the 70.3 triathlon qualifier for Ironman and I promised I'd go with her."

"You're competing?"

"No, just going to hang out and offer moral support. My triathlon days are over. You and Uncle Frank should come along if he feels up to it. It'll be like a party."

"We can't, I have too much to do to get ready for the wedding. And even though he looks pretty good, I have a feeling he's sicker than he's divulged. But tell Pua good luck for me."

36

It was Friday, the day before the triathlon, and Pua and Jessica had checked into the Hapuna Beach Hotel. Every year the race started at the south end of the beach fronting the resort. The race consisted of three legs, the first being the 1.2-mile swim, then the 56-mile bike race to Hawi and back, followed by the 13.1-mile run.

Gabbie had volunteered to take Henry for the night and Kainoa went fishing with Uncle Jack.

Since Henry was with Gabbie, and Sam was still shadowing Uncle Frank, he and Henry played video games and hung out while Gabbie and Uncle Frank were in another room picking out new drapes and furniture online. Their house had come fully furnished, but Uncle Frank told Gabbie to make it her own.

That evening, Pua and Jessica went to dinner at the Italian restaurant in the Queen's Marketplace, so Pua could load up on carbohydrates. The eatery was a few miles down the road from the hotel and was buzzing with athletes who were all there to pack on the carbs, for energy, the night before the big race.

As they walked in the door the smell of a combination of

garlic, tomatoes, baking bread, olive oil, and hot cheese filled their nostrils.

Jessica and Pua sat in a booth that had a view of the front door as they chatted about Pua's strategy for the race, while they waited for their dinners to arrive.

Jessica always sat with her back to the wall, with a view of the entrance, anytime she went into a restaurant. As a retired cop, she still practiced the habit every time she went out to eat, without even thinking about it.

Like muscle memory, every time the door opened, she glanced in that direction for a possible threat. Pua had noticed, a long time ago, that her sister had always done it and didn't think much of it, until the door opened again and, instead of glancing, Jessica focused on the man who'd come through the door.

Pua turned to see who she was looking at, and as she instantly recognized him, she just as quickly spun back around. She could only see his face, not what he was wearing, as only his head was visible above the booth that was blocking her viewpoint, but not Jessica's.

A sharp pain flashed in her gut, similar to the time when she'd been arrested by Detective Swanson months earlier.

"What the hell is he doing here?" she whispered to Jessica, as if he could hear her in a noisy room packed full of people eating.

Jessica grinned.

"It's not funny. I thought you said they couldn't arrest me again."

Jessica watched Swanson as he followed the hostess to a table alone, and jutted her chin toward him. Pua fought the urge to look but had to. He'd come in from a bike ride and had his cycling gear on that consisted of black bib shorts and a bright red shirt that hugged his upper body. His legs and arms were tanned and muscular and Pua had a hard time taking her eyes off of him.

She had a sigh of relief, "I thought he was here to arrest me. I know it's not rational and I didn't do anything, but still, that initial feeling of fear just popped up. It doesn't make any sense."

"I get that sense of fear every time I get a letter from the IRS, or I open the electric bill," Jessica joked.

When Detective Swanson first sat down at the table, he was pointed toward a wall. After the hostess handed him the menu and left, he changed his mind and moved to the opposite side of the table, with a view of the entire room. It was only a minute before he noticed Pua sitting across the room—their eyes locked, and he smiled.

It was at that point, the waiter brought Jessica pasta primavera and Pua had lasagna. "I love Italian food," Jessica said, after she forked the first bite of the savory vegetables.

"That's the only reason I compete. Just so I can eat pasta," Pua said, as she tried to ignore Swanson while she ate.

They were halfway through dinner when he got up and walked over to their table.

"He's coming this way," Pua said, just before she took another bite of lasagna. Her pulse began to rise as he made his way toward her. She smiled when he stopped in front of the table, as she tried to swallow. Her cheeks felt warm and she blushed as she introduced him to Jessica. "This is Detective Swanson, he's the one who arrested me," Pua said, as she smiled. He smiled back, "I'm glad to see you don't appear to be holding that against me."

"I'm not. Are you racing tomorrow?"

"Yes, and you?"

Pua nodded, as she fought the urge to look at more than just his face.

Swanson saw the waiter out of the corner of his eye. "I see the waiter bringing my dinner. Good luck tomorrow, Pua, and nice meeting you." He glanced at Jessica, as she nodded. Then his gaze returned to Pua, before he turned.

As he went back to his table, Pua said, with a devilish grin, "I'd let him put the handcuffs on me again."

The next morning the cannon sounded, and two thousand people raced toward the first buoy. Pua got a lousy start when she tangled with another swimmer and her goggles got knocked off.

"It's okay, swim your own race," she thought, as she tried to calm herself and make up the lost time, after getting her goggles back on. Once she got into a rhythm, she continued to count her strokes and began to gain on the leaders, as she pulled hard with each arm. Even with the goggles' setback, Pua had caught the leaders, on the final stretch, and moved into second place by the time she got back to the beach. Her training of a daily two-and-a-half-mile swim had paid off. Now it was time for the next leg of the race on the bike.

While Mother Nature had cooperated during the swim, with calm seas, the bike ride to Hawi was another story. The road the racers used to go to Hawi rimmed the base of the Kohala Mountains, and twenty mph wind gusts in the vicinity were the norm, but that day they were interspersed with gusts up to sixty mph. What Pua originally thought was going to be a walk in the park turned into a nightmare when she got blown off the road, from a gust, halfway to Hawi. She only suffered minor scrapes and bruises, and barely missed a big pile of lava rocks, when she crashed.

The front wheel of her bike was badly bent, and as she tried to straighten it with a rock, she heard a voice.

"Need a hand?"

She looked up and saw it was Detective Swanson. Pua grimaced and said, "I don't need a detective, I need a new wheel." She instantly regretted how snarky that sounded.

"You can call me Mike."

"I'm sorry Mike, that was uncalled for. I'm just frustrated; this is going to kill my chances to qualify for Ironman this year," she said, as she continued to pound on the wheel."

"Tell you what, I'm not trying to qualify. Let's switch front tires and you can get back in the race, and I'll wait for support with spare wheels. They should be along soon," he said, as he had already flipped his bike upside down to remove the tire.

"Are you sure?"

Mike nodded while he loosened the fasteners that held the wheel on.

Pua smiled again and said, "I'll owe you big time. How can I pay you back?"

"Dinner tonight after the race, and you can tell me how you did."

Pua started to remove her front tire, and said, "It's a date. Meet me in front of the Ruth Chris Steakhouse at seven." And she was back in the race, within minutes, as if she had only taken a short rest stop.

The remainder of the race was uneventful, and she came in third in her age group, which meant she'd qualified for Ironman later in the year.

❧

Mike was waiting in front of the restaurant when Pua arrived a few minutes before seven, which was an accomplishment for her. He had on khaki shorts and a black Tommy Bahama shirt and looked just the way Pua liked her men, casual, but dressy.

He smiled when he saw Pua come around the corner from the parking lot. She had on a red dress and a matching new pair of Manolo Blahnik pumps that she'd been waiting to wear for just such an occasion.

As they walked up the stairs to the restaurant, Mike placed his hand on the small of Pua's back. His touch was light, and she felt her loins start to warm. She couldn't remember the simple touch of a man who had made her feel that way–it had been a very long time.

After they were seated, Mike said, "I'm sorry I had to arrest you. Originally, I thought you did it. Later on, I wasn't so sure, and I wanted to keep investigating, but the higher-ups were adamant that we charge you."

Pua grinned, "I was going to pay the bill, but now I'm starting to think you should," and they laughed as they relaxed.

"I planned on paying anyway, since you said it was a date. Had you said you were just paying me back for swapping wheels, I'd let you pay," Mike smiled.

They were ravenous from the day's grueling activities and each had T-bone steaks, cooked to their likings, hers was medium rare, his rare.

"Just wipe its nose and run it by the fire," he told the waiter.

"Last night was pasta, tonight is steak–tomorrow I'm going on a diet," Pua said, as she spooned a bite of chocolate cake and vanilla ice cream into her new friend's mouth. When the waiter brought the bill Pua let Mike pay, but said he'd have to let her return the favor some other way, yet to be determined, and Mike agreed.

They finished dinner and dessert just in time to catch the hula show on the outdoor stage, a short way from the restaurant.

"I love watching hula," Mike said, as they watched the performers. Pua smiled and nodded. A few minutes later, the MC of the show asked if any of the ladies in the audience would like to come up on stage for the next hula. Pua smiled, slipped off her shoes, and handed them to Mike. "They're expensive, don't set them down." Mike nodded and smiled as he watched her go up on stage.

The MC recognized Pua, not from the trial, but from the

hula halau she used to dance with, that participated in the Merry Monarch Festival every year.

"Ladies and gentlemen, we have an extraordinary guest with us here tonight, Pua Murphy. She's well known in the hula world and retired from competition."

When the song Hanalei Moon started to play, it was just like Pua had never left the halau. Her hips moved to the rhythm of the song, as if they were one. The audience was mesmerized the entire four minutes and thirty-three seconds she danced to the song.

Mike walked Pua to her car after the show, and lightly kissed her on the lips goodbye, but not before he got her phone number, and they made plans to see each other again.

Jessica was sitting on the lanai when Pua got home.

As she stepped up on the lanai, Jessica asked, "How'd it go?"

"I wanted him to use those handcuffs of his on me...," she grinned. "But I'm going to resist the urge until at least the third date, and then it's going to be naked time," she said, as she went inside to take a cold shower.

37

<hr>

It was only a couple of days before the wedding, and Gabbie and Jessica met at Lava Java to have banana pancakes, and work on last-minute details that had yet to be taken care of.

After Gabbie handed Jessica a copy of the to-do list for the big day, she said, "I called O'Halleran this morning to invite him to the wedding, and he told me the latest about Larry being arrested for Erica's murder. He said he heard, from a friend in the department, that they got a witness who said he saw the whole thing from the Hele-On bus stop, across the street from the beach park. The witness also said it was too dark to identify the driver of the car, but he got the license plate. The guy said it was a vanity plate, so there was no way he was going to forget, 'MrBlack'."

Jessica stopped writing names to add to the guest list and put her pen down, and said, "The news on the way over here said they released Larry. What's up with that? Did O'Halleran say?"

"Larry had a solid alibi, his mistress swore he was with her during the time Erica's body got dumped. Larry's lawyer told Detective Swanson it was a setup, somebody had stolen the plate off Larry's car. So, they cut him loose for the time being," Gabbie paused for a second to take a sip of coffee, and said, "Isn't Swanson the guy Pua is dating?"

Jessica nodded and said, "Yes, she's in lust–or love, I can't quite tell yet. And she doesn't seem to mind that he put her in jail once. I think she's seriously into bondage, and took his previous action as foreplay," Jessica joked, and they both laughed.

Gabbie's phone buzzed and at first she glanced at the text, then studied it for a minute and her brow wrinkled. "I have to go in about fifteen minutes, Frank's plane will be landing in a half hour. He says he left Honolulu about ten minutes ago and will need a ride when he gets back. He's been over there all week having tests done. His doctor had him do a PET scan a few days ago, and he just got the results. It showed the spots of cancer he had earlier were continuing to shrink." Gabbie threw her phone into her purse. "I suspect he's never told me the truth about his condition, but it's only a hunch. Today I'm getting the truth," she said, as she shook her head.

"That's great news. Well, maybe not the part where he didn't tell you the whole story," Jessica said, as she leaned over and hugged Gabbie.

"Go get him, I got this," Jessica said, as she continued to work on the guest list with one hand, and fork bites of bananas and pancakes smothered in coconut syrup into her mouth with the other.

Gabbie hugged Jessica again and left for the airport.

After she picked up Frank, and they were on their way home, she said in her FBI serious voice, "I want the whole story, all of it. I've already been married to one lying bastard, I don't need two."

Uncle Frank had been a gambler all his life, and he knew it was time to show his cards. He cleared his throat, "Fair enough. When I left the mainland, the doctor in Kingman said I'd better get my affairs in order. He thought for certain I was going to die. But I look at doctors like mechanics, you just have to keep looking for the right one. So, I found one on Oahu that said he thought he could save me. He put me on yet another new, experimental medication and it worked. My cancer has gone into remission for real this time."

"So, you lied to me," she said, in a flat tone.

"Technically that's correct, I'm sorry honey. I just didn't want to see you upset. I'll never lie to you again. I promise."

Gabbie smiled and said, with a straight face, as she stared down the highway, "If you do, I'll switch your meds for placebos."

Unsure if she was joking or not, Uncle Frank shifted his eyes toward her and nodded.

38

———————

After Larry got released from the Kona jail, he went home to think about who might have set him up. He had a few names that came to mind, but after reviewing them, he was sure they would have just tried to kill him instead. That was the thing about laundering money for the Russian mob, they would never have gone to the trouble of trying to frame him. He knew if it was them, he'd already have been dead.

Larry grabbed a beer out of the refrigerator and went out to the lanai to sit and think while he stared at the ocean. He retraced his steps the entire week before Erica's body was found. The license plate was stolen from a car that hadn't been driven in a month.

During that time his BMW had been in the shop getting refurbished. The only time the car had been out of the shop was when he picked it up and drove it to the weekly real estate meeting held at a local restaurant in town.

Every real estate agent on the west side of the island went to the weekly caravan meeting before going out to look at a list of featured homes for sale. Larry determined it had to be there that someone stole the front plate from his car, but who?

And why would they want to kill Erica? He'd thought about killing her once or twice but nixed the idea when he thought he had successfully framed her for Charles' murder.

Larry knew the plate wasn't taken when the car was in the shop because it was still on the front bumper when he picked it up. He specifically remembered seeing the vanity plate as he walked by the front of the car, because he thought about switching it to his new BMW.

Larry swallowed the rest of his beer and drove to the parking lot of the restaurant, to look for surveillance cameras on any of the nearby buildings. It didn't take him long to find one. It was at a car dealer across the street, and he asked them to review the footage for the day he attended the caravan meeting. The used car manager stuffed a hundred dollar tip in his pocket after he found what Larry was looking for. The video clearly showed the real estate agent who stole his license plate.

After Larry got a copy of the video he went out to his car and called his lawyer.

"Tanner Hawthorne, that's the son-of-a-bitch who stole the plate off my BMW," he said.

"You have the video?" the lawyer asked.

"I do, I'll email it to you right now."

"Excellent, I'll let Detective Swanson know. This should get him off your back."

Larry hung up and went to make funeral arrangements for Erica.

39

The day of the wedding, scattered showers were forecast for the island. Uncle Frank and Gabbie decided that morning, the wedding on the beach would take place, rain or shine.

Sam and Uncle Frank were the first to walk the sandy trail to the small beach, at the end of the runway of the Old Kona Airport. Uncle Frank was getting around better than he had in the last nine months.

He and Sam met the officiant Gabbie had found on the internet. Gabbie had told Uncle Frank the guy was some kind of new-age reverend and the only one available, on such short notice, to perform the ceremony. The officiant had arrived early and was busy spreading crystals around the beach.

After a few minutes of talking with him about how the ceremony was going to go down, Uncle Frank offered the man a Tic Tac.

"No, thanks, those things are full of chemicals," he said.

Uncle Frank smiled and said, "You have the breath of a buzzard, take one, I insist," and Uncle Frank held out the small container of breath mints again.

The man paused, but sensed Uncle Frank wasn't to be

messed with, and slowly opened his hand so Uncle Frank could drop one in, and then he put it in his mouth.

Uncle Jack had been mingling and took a nip from his flask from time to time to take the edge off. After he witnessed the exchange between the reverend and Uncle Frank, he offered them both a swig.

"Don't tempt me," Uncle Frank replied and smiled. The internet reverend was happy to take a long pull off the flask and Uncle Frank gave him another breath mint, which he didn't resist.

"What's up with Frank, he's tight as a banjo string," Uncle Jack whispered in Sam's ear.

Sam whispered back, "He's sober, seventy, and he's never been married before."

"Ahh, poor bastard, I guess I'll quit offering him alcohol," Uncle Jack muttered and wandered off down the beach.

About twenty friends and family had gathered on the beach to wait for the ceremony. Sam was the best man, Jessica the maid of honor and Henry the ring bearer. Pua had brought three big bags full of red and pink plumeria flowers and spread them in a circle on the sand near the water's edge.

Grady O'Halleran had agreed to give the bride away and waited at the parking lot at the trailhead for Gabbie to arrive, so he could walk her down the sandy path to the beach.

Pua was in charge of the music and kept a sharp eye toward the parking lot, so when she saw Grady start to walk Gabbie down the path, she could hit the play button on the CD player she had brought. The song Gabbie had chosen was "Over the Rainbow" by Brother Iz.

People continued to mingle until Kainoa started yelling, "They're here, they're here," and Pua said, "Okay, okay," and held up her finger to her mouth, as she looked at him.

Everyone moved into place around the circle of flowers as Gabbie and Jessica got out of the 4Runner. Gabbie waited until Jessica was at the makeshift altar on the beach before she and Grady came down the path.

O'Halleran was hardly noticeable in contrast to Gabbie as he accompanied her to the beach. She was adorned with a haku made with an assortment of Hawaiian flowers, interwoven with baby's breath, and wore a white traditional Hawaiian style wedding dress.

Everyone watched as O'Halleran walked Gabbie down the sandy trail. It was a beautiful ceremony at the water's edge, with everyone gathered around.

Uncle Frank wore a maile lei over his white Tommy Bahama shirt, with white slacks, and as he stood next to Gabbie, they looked like the perfect couple. During the ceremony, a blessing of light sprinkles fell on the couple as the officiant pronounced them husband and wife, and then subsided.

After the ceremony was over, Uncle Frank tipped the officiant an extra hundred bucks, because he felt bad about the buzzard comment he made earlier.

The only hitch in the ceremony was when Henry dropped the wedding ring in the sand, and in the shuffle to pick it up, it got pushed underneath the surface and it took a minute to find.

Everyone gathered for photos on the beach and then left for the reception, except for Frank and Gabbie. They stayed behind to take sunset photos and would join everyone later.

The reception was held in the courtyard of the main house on Uncle Frank and Gabbie's ninety-acre coffee estate, in Holualoa. Guests mingled while they waited for Gabbie and Uncle Frank to arrive.

Uncle Jack and Grady stood on the lanai of the main house, and admired the view, while they sipped twelve-year-old Irish whisky that O'Halleran had brought. They compared war stories from their long careers in law enforcement and reminisced about a couple of cases they'd worked together in Honolulu, that involved both agencies they'd worked for.

O'Halleran had been with the Honolulu PD just over twenty years, before he'd moved to the Big Island to work with Jessica and Gabbie on the serial killer task force two years earlier.

Uncle Jack had two decades of service with Naval Intelligence, at Pearl Harbor, before moving to Kona to retire and start a charter fishing business.

"I'm still tuned into what's going on around here even though I retired recently," Grady said.

"Do you have any intel on the status of Larry Black's case?" Uncle Jack asked.

"He's off the hook. His lawyer showed up at the station yesterday with a video that exonerated Black, as far as dumping the body was concerned. One of his real estate pals tried to frame him. The guy stole the plate off one of Larry's cars, and put it on his, before he went to dump Erica Black's body down at Kahaluu. Larry recognized the guy in the video and identified him."

While Grady paused to take another sip of whiskey, Uncle Jack shook his head, "So he wasn't involved at all?"

"Nope, they picked up the guy in the video, and he confessed. He said it was an accident that happened when he and Erica were having sex. They were into some kinky shit where he'd choke her to get off. I guess he took it too far that time. At least that's the story he told detectives. My buddy in Vice said they didn't buy it and signed him up for second degree murder."

Uncle Jack shook his head again, "Larry Black is like Teflon, nothing sticks to that guy. I've been watching him for a couple of years, waiting to see him get locked up—maybe someday. Did the guy happen to say why he tried to frame Larry?"

O'Halleran nodded as he poured them both more whiskey.

"Because Larry screwed him in a deal a while back, and he thought it was a good way to give him some payback.

I'm not surprised Erica was murdered. I'm just surprised it wasn't Larry who did it."

Their conversation was interrupted by the sound of a silver spoon being tapped on the side of a glass, in the courtyard, announcing that the dinner buffet was ready. Any further pontification about what should've happened in the life of Larry and Erica Black would have to wait.

The guests gorged on a luau style menu with three main courses of kalua pig, prime rib, and fresh Ono. Sam and Jessica sat next to each other at the family table, with Henry next to Sam.

After dinner, as Sam and Jessica watched Uncle Frank and Gabbie have their first dance, Sam whispered to Jessica "When are you coming home?"

She answered his question with one of her own, "When do you have a year of being clean?"

"Three months," he said.

"That's your answer."

40

THREE MONTHS LATER

Uncle Frank's latest PET scan was negative, and his cancer was still in remission. He and Gabbie had agreed to put off their honeymoon cruise around the world for three months, until after Sam's first anniversary of being drug free. Uncle Frank said it was either that, or they would have to bring him along.

It was a Saturday night NA meeting and every week they celebrated birthdays with a cake. And every week Sam and Uncle Frank attended, since they had returned from Laughlin.

When the secretary of the meeting asked for a volunteer to make coffee before the start of the meeting, Uncle Frank nudged Sam.

Sam still didn't volunteer and whispered to Uncle Frank, "You know who I am right?"

And Uncle Frank quickly whispered back, "Yeah, a guy that almost died from a drug overdose. It'll be good for you, people that make coffee usually don't relapse." Sam reluctantly raised his hand and took the job.

When the leader of the meeting asked if there were any birthdays, Sam and a couple of other people got up and came to the front of the room, as was customary in that meeting.

Sam had the least amount of time clean and was the first to receive a metal coin, about the size of a half dollar, that had a Latin numeral 1 on it. Around the edge of the coin was the inscription "To thine own self be true."

He stared at the coin for a moment, and then looked up at the members in the audience. There were about thirty people in the room, and he looked over at Uncle Frank, and said, "Thanks for not giving up on me."

He scanned the faces around the room looking back at him, and he saw Jessica standing in the back of the room. Their eyes locked, his filled with tears, and his voice cracked as he said, "Thank you." And he stepped aside, so the guy with two years could get his chip and say a few words.

After the meting was over, people came up and congratulated Sam and shook his hand. A young man who'd identified earlier in the meeting, with less than thirty days clean, asked Sam if he'd be his sponsor–Sam nodded and gave him his phone number. He shook a couple more hands and went to look for Jessica at the back of the room. His heart sank when he couldn't find her, she had left.

Uncle Frank and Sam talked in the parking lot for a while before they left to go home. "Don't rush her, she'll come around when she's ready," was Uncle Frank's advice.

Sam thought about Jessica the whole time, as he drove along the coast on the way home. He couldn't understand why she'd come to the meeting and then left before it was over.

It was a full moon and Sam stopped at Lyman's Bay on the way home, to watch the moonlight reflect off the ocean as small waves rolled into the shoreline. The moonlight on the water had a calming effect, but he was still sad from not being able to see Jessica after the meeting.

He said the serenity prayer to himself and continued on his way home to yet another night alone. A few miles later, when he rounded the corner to the house on Keauhou Bay, there were cars parked up and down the street on the shoulder. He thought, "Hmm, someone's having a party." Then he saw her as he rolled up to the driveway. Jessica stood at the edge and held Henry's hand as Sam turned the truck toward them, and stopped short as he parked half in the driveway and half in the street. He jumped out of the truck, and in nothing flat, he rounded the hood of the truck and embraced Jessica and Henry. The three of them hugged, and hugged some more, before going inside. Sam and Jessica both had tears in their eyes, as Henry stared at them for a minute and began to look concerned, until they reassured him they were tears of joy–and there was nothing to worry about.

Uncle Frank had distracted Sam after the meeting, while a lot of people from the meeting, and friends and family, had gone to Sam and Jessica's house for a surprise party she had put together.

Pilau was back on his perch in the living room entertaining everyone with some of his more colorful vocabulary, and Mr. Jangles was back to staring at Pilau and wondering what he might taste like.

The same suitcases Jessica had packed when she'd left and took Henry had been put back in their respective bedrooms and unpacked. Happiness and laughter once again filled their home… and sorrow and pity had been left behind.

The End.

Free Prequel Death in Hawaii

ALSO BY J.E. TRENT

Prequel to book 1. Death in Hawaii Get this prequel for free when you join my email list. It's the only place it's available.- **Click here.**

Hawaii Thriller Series

Book 1 Death in Paradise

Book 2 Death Orchid

Book 3 The Kona Strangler

ABOUT THE AUTHOR

J.E. Trent

J.E. Trent lived full time in Hawaii for over twenty two years and loves sharing his knowledge of the tropical paradise in his novels.

Hawi
Honokaa
Waimea
Mauna Kea
Hilo
Kona
Hawaii
Pahoa
Captain
Cook
Mauna Loa
Mountain
View
Pahala
Naalehu

Kauai
Kekaha
Kapaa
Lihue
Puuwai
Niihau
Oahu
Pearl City
Honolulu
Molokai
Kaunakakai
Maui
Lanai
Wailuku
Red Hill
Hana
Kahoolawe
Hawi
Honokaa
Waimea
Mauna Kea
Hilo
Kailua
Hawaii
Pahoa
Captain Cook
Mauna Loa
Mountain View
Pahala
Naalehu
PACIFIC OCEAN
HAWAII

ACKNOWLEDGMENTS

A Big Mahalo to Judith Shaw and my wife, Eila, for the final edit. It was only because of their input that this story came out as well as it did. I'm truly blessed to have their kokua. (help)

Shane Rutherford at Dark Moon Graphics made the beautiful cover for the book.

Mahalo to all the authors who have shared their knowledge at kboards.com and the 20BooksTo50K Facebook group and many others.

AFTERWORD

At the time when I got the idea for Sam and Jessica I had been an auto mechanic for about thirty-five years. I was over fifty and my body was screaming at me every morning that I'd better find another way to make a living. Around that time I had written some flash fiction that I had gotten a lot of positive feedback on and thought with some study that maybe I could write a novel.

After a lot of brainstorming, Sam and Jessica came to be. A billionaire super yacht builder and a retired LA detective. They aren't perfect; they're growing through problems in their lives that people can relate to. They have character defects just like everybody does. But it's how they strive to overcome them and do the right thing, is what I hope to convey in their stories going forward in the Death in Hawaii Series.

During the twenty-two years I lived on the big island, I witnessed some amazing things. Those events are where a lot of the inspiration I get comes from. My goal is to intersperse those moments in my books creating something unique that you can only get when you read my stories.

Hawaii is a magical place, my words will never do it justice. I hope that readers take away a bit of aloha after spending time with Sam and Jessica.

Get the free prequel and new release notifications.

https://readerlinks.com/l/965413

HAWAIIAN GLOSSARY

Mana (Ma-Na)

Spirit

Aina (Eye-Na)

Land of the island.

Beach Boys

They light the resort's tiki torches, pull the pig from the imu and help tourists safely enjoy the beach.

Honu (Ho-Nu)

It is a green sea turtle.

Malama (Ma-La-ma)

To take care of.

Hapa (Ha-Pa)

Means mixed race. Hawaiian, Chinese, Japanese, Portuguese and Filipino make up the majority of the population in Hawaii and when they marry their children are called hapa. A mixture.

Huli-huli chicken is grilled on a trailer in a parking lot or on the side of the road. It's usually related to a fundraiser.

Da-Kine (dah-KINE) is a fill in word used for anything you can't remember the name of.

Aloha (ah-LOH-hah)

Aloha is "hello" and "goodbye." You could also have the spirit of aloha = Giving, caring.

Mahalo (mah-HA-loh)

Means "thank you."

Haole (HOW-leh)

It's used to refer to white people. It can be used offensively, but isn't always meant to be insulting. Originally it meant foreigner, but I seriously doubt anyone uses it for that anymore.

Kane (KAH-neh)

Kane refers to men or boys.

Wahine (wah-HEE-neh)

Wahine refers to women or girls.

Keiki (KAY-kee)

This word means "child." You may hear locals call their children "keiki."

Hale (HAH-leh)

Hale translates to "home" or "house." It can often refer to housing in general.

Pau (POW)

When you put the soy sauce bottle down, you may hear a local ask, "Are you pau with that?" Pau essentially means "finished" or "done."

Howzit (HOW-zit)

In Hawaii, "howzit" is a common pidgin greeting that translates to "hello" or "how are you?"

Lolo (loh-loh)

When someone calls you "lolo," they're saying you're "crazy or dumb." It's sometimes used in a teasing manner.

Ono (OH-noh)

Ono means "delicious." It can often be paired with the pidgin word "grinds," which translates to "food." So, if you eat something delicious, you might say it's ono grinds.

Ohana (oh-HAH-nah)

Means family.

Tita (tit-uh)

Refers to a woman or teenage girl who could be said to either be a tomboy or else somewhat aggressive, tough, or rough with her language or manners.

Tutu (too-too)

Means grand mother. Google says it references both grand parents, but I've never heard that on the island.

COPYRIGHT

www.ingramcontent.com/pod-product-compliance
Lightning Source LLC
Chambersburg PA
CBHW021335190726
48288CB00003B/1121